Penguin Books
Beard's Roman Women

Anthony Burgess was born in Manchester in 1917 and is
a graduate of the University there. After six years
in the Army he worked as an instructor for the Central
Advisory Council for Forces Education, as a college lecturer
in Speech and Drama and as a grammar school master.
From 1954 to 1960 he was an education officer
in the Colonial Service, stationed in Malaya and Borneo.

He became a full-time writer in 1960, though he had
already by then published three novels and a history of
English literature. A late starter in the art of fiction,
he had previously spent much creative energy on music,
and has composed many full-scale works for orchestra
and other media. His Third Symphony was performed
in the U.S.A. in 1975.

Anthony Burgess believes that in the fusion of musical
and literary form lies a possible future for the novel. His
Napoleon Symphony attempts to impose the shape of
Beethoven's 'Eroica' on the career of the Corsican
conqueror. His other books include *The Malayan Trilogy*; the
Enderby novels (including *The Clockwork Testament*);
Tremor of Intent; *Shakespeare*, a biography intended to act
as a foil to his Shakespeare novel, *Nothing Like the Sun*;
Honey for the Bears; *The Wanting Seed*; *MF*; *Urgent
Copy*; *ABBA ABBA*; *A Clockwork Orange*, made into
a film classic by Stanley Kubrick; *Ernest Hemingway and
His World*; and *1985*.

Mr Burgess lives with his second wife and his son in
France, Monaco and Italy, but mostly on the road in a
Bedford Dormobile.

Anthony Burgess

Beard's Roman Women

Penguin Books

Penguin Books Ltd, Harmondsworth,
Middlesex, England
Penguin Books, 625 Madison Avenue,
New York, New York 10022, U.S.A.
Penguin Books Australia Ltd, Ringwood,
Victoria, Australia
Penguin Books Canada Ltd, 2801 John Street,
Markham, Ontario, Canada L3R 1B4
Penguin Books (N.Z.) Ltd, 182–190 Wairau Road,
Auckland 10, New Zealand

First published in Great Britain by Hutchinson & Co. 1977
Published in Penguin Books 1979

Made and printed in Great Britain by
Richard Clay (The Chaucer Press) Ltd,
Bungay, Suffolk
Set in Intertype Lectura

To Liana

One

In the rainy March of 196– he had, an hour or so before being driven to the airport, cast his remaining metal lire into the Trevi fountain, daring Rome to call him back again. Not that Rome had really called him on this occasion: a matter only, or at least that had been the intention, of a few days' stopover on the way home to London from Brunei, via Singapore. He considered that he detested Rome, meaning its bloody history, its cowardly citizens, its godless bishops who were also godless popes, its boastful baroque, its insipid cuisine, its sour wine. A venal city and a cruel city and a city of robbers. Here his wife Leonora had had her first liver collapse and had loosed black blood over the hotel bedroom. She had spent time in a Roman hospital and had had Roman blood pumped into her. A city of robbers, even at the most rarefied professional level.

She died in an English March. He should have known, those quiet years in London when he was earning their living as a writer of scripts for radio, television and cinema, what her trouble was. He had even written a television play in which one of the characters, a writer of scripts for radio, television and cinema, died of cirrhosis. From those years in Brunei on, when he had worked for Radio Brunei, it never seemed to him that either of them drank excessively. In the tropics, surely, you sweated all that gin out before it got anywhere near the liver. To the house in Hammersmith they had had, true, one dozen bottles of Gordon's delivered weekly, but they dispensed tropical hospitality even to the delivery man; they drank wine only with dinner and did not invariably take a liqueur after;

they spent no more than two hours a day in pubs. He had emerged undamaged from this; why not then she also?

He realized too late what should always have been self-evident: that a woman was a smaller vessel than a man, that no man had a right to expect a woman, however much a woman wished it, to be a real, meaning drink for drink, companion. Add to this something always vaguely known: that white women living in the tropics suffered more than men from vitamin B deficiency; you then had reason enough for the decay of her liver. But even after the next, more massive, portal haemorrhage, when the hepatologist said 'If she drinks again she will die,' neither of them had been disposed to utter, outside a context of fiction or literary history, the dread word the doctors themselves had not uttered. Cirrhosis was for his television character, Caradoc Williams, or for Dick Tarleton of the Queen's Men. It was not for him, hence how could it be for her? There were medical dictionaries on his reference shelf, and these would have given him, had he cared to look, a candid reading of the signs. 'If she drinks again she will die.' That too was something for a television play.

The signs? Dulling of the eyes and hair, drying and yellowing of the skin, wasting of the limbs, grotesque distension of the abdomen. No notable loss of appetite, no pain, no impairment of memory or of intelligence. No sexual needs, apparently, but for some years now they had kept to their separate bedrooms, extolling the beauties of companionate love. A companionate life, call it, she sitting with her library novel by the electric fan, he clacking away at a script on the cleared dining-table. He shopped, she cooked. At the beginning of the terminal phase she, if not he, drank little enough. It was not that she was taking note of the hepatologist's warning: she did not care for the taste of blood in her mouth. 'Like,' she said more than once, 'regurgitating beef extract.' So strong drink would bring on another haemorrhage, and that would be another nuisance, what with having to wear a hospital nightgown again, be forbidden to smoke, be fed with the blood of strangers.

So she drank Schweppes tonic water well zested with lemon peel, but later said to hell, put a gin in, a single not a double, one single gin or so a day can do no harm. A glass of dry white wine can do no harm, nor a chilled lager, chilled things are good for the stomach. Then *Time-Life* held a great, somehow definitive, party in their building in Bruton Street, and to this even script-writers were invited, along with their wives. Of course, she had to go. She looked well, knocking back the generous rummers of gin, talking vigorously to Lady Snow and Lord Snowdon and the Leader of the Opposition, her dulled hair masked by an expensive golden wig, her face restored by cunning cosmesis to its former beauty, her swollen body tented in an elegant gold-thread caftan. Three days later the final portal haemorrhage began. The doctor was slow in arriving. Saucepans and jugs could scarcely keep pace with the tides of black blood. The doctor came at last and was grave and urgent. She was rushed into a hospital in Ealing.

While she was there, first transfused, then incised, a message came to him from his agent, announcing that Warner Brothers in Burbank, California, were anxious for him to fly over there and discuss the writing of a script for a very big film.

'Mr Schaumwein. He says you've already met.'

'It must have been at that *Time-Life* party. A fat man?'

'A fat voice. It's a musical they have in mind. He had that thing you did for the BBC about Shelley and Byron and Frankenstein and so on specially screened.'

'A *musical*? About *that*?'

'Well, Byron and Shelley and Mary Shelley and that Swiss lake they all lived near that summer, whenever it was. When she wrote *Frankenstein* and the others just wrote poetry. Somebody as the idea of doing a sort of ballet dream sequence with Frankenstein in it.'

'Interesting, but I can't go now. Leonora's very ill.'

'Will she be ill for long, do you think? They're very anxious to start talking about it.'

'They've pumped blood in and they've cut something out,

the spleen I think, and she just lies there, yellow and coma-
tose.'

'I see. Well, I'll let them know the position. Do you know
anything about musicals? *Their* musicals?'

'I saw that thing they did based on *Playboy of the Western
World*. With the dream leprechaun ballet sequence. Too much
whimsy, I thought.'

'Percy's on at their theatre in Leicester Square. Go and see
that if you can.'

'Percy? Who's Percy?'

'*Percy*. The title. About the boy looking for the Holy Grail.
And the man who fishes all day and the man with the garden
that's really a sort of brothel.'

'I'll try. Look, I'm really interested, tell them, but I do have
this problem. Parsifal is the name, really. Let them know
what the position is, will you?'

'I'll try.'

Two afternoons later Leonora seemed somewhat better.
They had feared brain damage, but she was reading the *Daily
Mirror* when he went up to her bed, and she said: 'This boy
of five raped.'

'You seem better, dear.' But the yellowness was astonishing.
A gaggle of Chinese nurses came in, on a visit from Singapore,
and they quacked astonishment at the yellowness. They were
in the charge of one of the resident sisters. He shooed them
away. 'I don't consider this to be really decent,' he said.

'What you consider is neither here nor there,' said the sister.
But then Leonora, in Kuo-Yü with very accurate intonation, told
them to bugger off. She seemed better. He told her about
Warner Brothers. She showed languid interest.

'So I thought I'd go and see this film tonight. Have dinner
out somewhere first. I miss your cooking.'

'I'd like dinner too. But they just drip this glucose into me.
And I'm so tired.'

'That's the effort of speaking Chinese perhaps. Anyway, I'll
telephone when I get back from the cinema.'

'I'm so tired all the time.'

The film was not good. The Fisher King had a song about fishing and wishing, and Percy, a blond rather silly youth, had something *alla marcia* in which he announced that he would not fail to find the trail that led to the Holy Grail, and there was sticky love-stuff for Klingsor's magic garden. Still, he could see what they might probably want for their film on the lovers of the lake (not a bad title, that), and he mused on it, as also on how long it would be before Leonora was better, over three double gins in a noisy Leicester Square pub. Back home in Hammersmith he telephoned the hospital. There was no change, they said: she was sleeping comfortably. He went to bed.

At two-thirty-five, blackness and noisy rain, the bedside telephone rang. It pierced a seemingly pointless dream about Rome in the rain (Grail, Waste Land, pope, redemption?).

'Mr Beard?' A man's voice, Ceylonese, Dr Lalkaka or something.

'Speaking.'

'Mrs Beard is – You had better come over.'

'She's –?'

'You had better come over immediately.' While he dressed, a vapid song started up in his brain, about Rome in the rain, I'll never see you again, You brought me sorrow and pain, Rome in the Rome in the rain. That was stupid. Rome could not be blamed all that much. She had collapsed, true, on the wet cobbles somewhere near the Isola Tiberina, and people had said *ubriaca ubriaca*, meaning drunk. Unsympathetic and unhelpful bastards, not even willing to help to lift her to her feet or call a taxi. But it could have been like that anywhere. He was trying to call a taxi now, or a minicab, anything, but it seemed hopeless. It was after five, the first day of spring as he noted from the Snoopy calendar behind the little living-room bar from which he was doing the telephoning, an anniversary easy to remember, meet for a Victorian poem, why did she die with the daffodils, but also black wet night and no

11

taxis anywhere. Stay: there was one radio-cab delivering a fare to Hounslow; that would come for him; about forty minutes; what was the address again? My wife's dying. Sorry about that, guv, but we're doing our best, console yourself by reflecting that nobody can't do nothing about it, don't blame yourself if you don't get there in time.

He shaved with his battery-razor, prowling the long room. On the dining-table just by the kitchen door lay the Olivetti Lettera 32, folio 45 of a script in it, something for television, the mouth of the speaker frozen open in mid-speech. Compassionately, he clacked the speech to its end and shut the mouth. 'The whole bloody world turned into a dungy farmyard, clucking politicians that lay no eggs, a donkey braying from a field like a threat of recession.' Shit. The taxi was throbbing outside.

In the taxi, he rehearsed lines, Let go, let go, darling, death's nothing to fear, here he is, he's gentle enough, a smooth driver to wherever you're going, go with him smiling. Ronald Beard as inept psychopomp. But when he got to her she was beyond seeming to swallow, in the final gasps for air he had envisaged, such sub-Huxleyan treacle. They had moved her from her middle place in the long ward to a private room at the end of it. She glowed with an old-guinea patina in the dim light, a few shallow breaths from the end. He waited about three minutes to confirm that he was now Ronald Beard the widower.

Next morning he would have to come back to collect her rings and see about the death certificate. Meanwhile he was to go home again in the rain and wait for the dawn and a reasonable hour to start telephoning relatives and friends. I fear (enjoying it really) I've some bad news for you. The taxi had a radio that played pop-music. Beard didn't really mind, but new widowhood conferred certain rights worth taking just because they were rights. When a pop-group called the Grateful Dead was announced he asserted his rights. The driver was grumpy, having his rights too, but he yielded.

A week later the cremation took place at Mortlake. He had

meanwhile stripped the house of most of the things she had worn and taken them to a local voluntary organization that distributed such needments to the poor. Not all that poor, really, however poor they were, since they were still alive. He began to understand too about ghosts now, for he heard her cough come from the bathroom and saw her, for half a second, sitting in her accustomed chair. He was lonely as hell, despite knocks on the door from women he did not know but who assured him that they were neighbours – widows and divorcees and two women who said that they hated their husbands, all asking, leering sympathetically the while, if they could be of any help. The cremation was the regular sort of cremation regularly ignited by the local funeral directors, with 'The God of Love My Shepherd Is' on tape and a few brisk words from the resident non-sectarian clergyman on the laughably self-evident truth of the doctrine of the resurrection of the body. Then relatives and friends went away with relics of the deceased – a beaver coat, a pair of calfskin boots, gold and silver, a just-started bottle of High and Dry. He was lonely as hell again.

He was also fifty. They had been married for twenty-six years. He had got out of the habit of sex. Ready enough for infidelity for his health's sake, he had feared that the time for being unfaithful might also be the time for her to give out blood again and him to start living forever in guilt. There was also the question of cooking. She had cooked well in the plain Welsh fashion, but here he was cracking hard-boiled eggs over the kitchen sink. The *Bon Viveur* page in the *Daily Telegraph* showed him how to cook veal in Marsala and, since the Marsala was open and not all used up, a *zabaglione* for afters. Eating, he remembered that Leonora and he had eaten this very same meal, though with artichokes added, just before her collapse in rainy Rome, and that she had irritated him by pronouncing *zabaglione* with a hard *g*.

'That's wrong,' he said. 'An insult to the language.'

'Insult my arse. It's a question of who's to be master, mistress if you like, you or the language. Insult, indeed.'

'That's stupid, and you know it.'

'Would you like this *zabag*,' she said softly, '*lione* thrown in your fucking face?'

Always quick on the draw, Welsh blood. After lunch he played Schoenberg on the hi-fi. She had always hated Schoenberg. Turn that fucking noise off. Or, alternatively: You know I'm not well and that music gives me a headache. Have you no consideration at all? But now he could play *Moses and Aaron* as loud as he wished. No, he could not: there was admonitory banging on the neighbour wall. Rid yourself of one circumscription of liberty and there was always another waiting. A good phrase: he must try it out on Leonora. Ah, classical situation: there was a sonnet by Wordsworth on that theme: *Surprised by joy, impatient as the wined*. He dined on what he had lunched on, thus finishing the Marsala. He went to his local pub, the Three Feathers, played darts, got more or less drunk. He was in bed at eleven-twenty, asleep at eleven-twenty-five.

At two-thirty-five, blackness and noisy rain, the bedside telephone rang. His luminous watch told him, as before, the time. He lay quite unable to move. The ringing continued. He could not answer it. It was all going to happen all over again: the two weeks since that other call had become a kind of film loop, and now his life was to be a living through of the same sequence, over and over, once he picked up that receiver. The ringing stopped at last, the minute hand moved on, he was probably safe. He switched on the lamp, lighted a Schimmelpenninck Duet, read what he had written of his new television play, his heart pounding but that may have been chiefly the drink, including the Marsala, did not much like what he had written. 'I've lived with you for ten years, and Christ alone knows how I've done it. Each time you make that little double grunting noise prefatory to some weighty borborygm I've heard a million times before I want to scream. I want to scream and scream and scream and –' The telephone rang again. Three-twelve. It would surely be all right this time. He lifted the receiver and found California frying away on the line. The hunters are up in America. A hard female voice, like frozen orange juice, asked him if he was Mr Beard. Mr Schaumwein for you, sir. Go ahead.

'You've had one hell of a time, Ron, we know, so we want you out here. Talk about the project. London office has been informed, Jack Mohammed there will make all arrangements. Start living again, boy, death is crap.'

'Did you ring before? About forty minutes ago?'

'Call before? Was he called before, Helen, about forty minutes? No, nobody called you before, Ron, not from this office, guess you must have been having, what the hell they call it, a pree money tory dream, you were asleep, right?'

'Thank you. Thank you very much. And I'll remember what you said. About death being a load of crap, I mean.'

'You do that.' And without valediction, the Hollywood manner as he was to learn, Beard was hung up on. The loop was snipped and spliced into the great reel of continuing life. That was too banal, he reflected, even for a television play. That earlier call had evidently been a wrong number.

The plane from Heathrow to Los Angeles had one intermediate stop, this being at Chicago's O'Hare airport, where the entire crew changed. The new stewardesses in first class were dressed alluringly but bizarrely as microskirted beefeaters complete with ruff and royal monogram. Their pants, as he clearly saw them when one called Janie leaned over to serve a martini to a window-seat, were patterned with the union jack. The airline was inaugurating, this very day, an in-flight fantasy series service called The Best of Both Transworlds, and it was beginning with a gastric parody of Great Britain – 'not,' said the silk-tasselled handout, 'the old stuffy pip-pip image but the new swinging Carnaby Street Tom Jones one.' Beard was served with strong Milwaukee ale in a plastic tankard which he could keep if he wished as a souvenir of Jollie Olde, and with what was called a pub lunch of mild shrimp curry with salad and thousand-island dressing. On succeeding flights, he read, there would be France ('Oo la la, you fly wiz to me to gay Paree, n'est-

ce pas'), Italy ('you like-a munch-a da spaghett and hear-a da music of Joe Green, Giuseppe Verdi to you') and Manhattan Penthouse, which might or might not be more authentic. After lunch, one of the delectable beefeaters served him Beefeater gin and tonic all the way to Los Angeles, so that he was drunk when he entered the waiting studio car under the golden smog. Death was crap, right.

Ed Schaumwein said that again at the end of their tourist visit to Forest Lawn. This was intended to put Leonora's death in its proper perspective by demonstrating that death was also an aspect of life, or else life an aspect of death, something like that. Beard saw a sunset-glow blow-up of Leonardo da Vinci's 'Last Supper' and heard an oleaginous recorded commentary. He visited the cemetery store, which sold plastic statuettes of David and the Three Graces and little girls with their skirts blown up by the wind. He very nearly put down a deposit for his eventual inurnment in Poet's Corner. 'Don't be in too much of a hurry,' advised Ed Schaumwein. 'You have a real Poet's Corner back there in Westminster Church. You may make it there, boy, and nothing to pay.' Ed Schaumwein was a formidable man like Genghis Khan and had, indeed, played that role along with many others before turning producer. He was also a hearty eater, and they had a hot pastrami sandwich at a place ouside the cemetery gates called The Last Chance. The important thing for Ron, asserted Ed Schaumwein, was to start to live again, meaning work a little and get laid a lot.

'I'm afraid I've rather lost touch with that kind of thing.'

Ed Schaumwein showed chewed hot pastrami in disbelief. Beard explained it all, the avoidance of guilt, the superiority of marriage as complex semiotics to mere sex, hence hence hence – That was crap and he knew it. 'Crap and you know it,' Ed Schaumwein said. 'You're going to get laid.'

In Schaumwein's office at Warner Brothers in Burbank, more of a bar than an office, they discussed the film project unsystematically but creatively, meaning drunkenly. Sometimes the Head of Scripts was there, a fierce sober man who talked much about Motivation, and sometimes George Roy Hill, a rising young director who had studied music under Hindemith and written a thesis on *Finnegans Wake*. The project had had its beginnings at a Hollywood party at which Paul Newman or someone similar had said he'd like to play Lord Byron, great handsome limping lecher or layer, also poet, and had then gone into a claudicant exophthalmic routine which Joanne Woodward said was worthier of Frankenstein, meaning his monster. The laughter aroused by what seemed to all present, except one, the total improbability of this collocation was, or would have been at a soberer gathering, quenched by this one, a morose rewrite man, who told them all seriously that Byron had probably given serious rewrite advice to the authoress of *Frankenstein*, and then recounted to whomever would listen the whole story of that creative summer by the waters of Leman. So one thing had led to another, many a true word spoken in, and here they were, Ron and Ed, with the water sprinklers making rainbows on the lawns without and the smog all golden above, being creative.

When they were not being creative, there was drinking and dining at the Brown Derby, the Bistro, Chasen's, with dear Ed and Molly, Ed's wife, a charming strawberry blonde given, in a well-groomed way, to Zen and astrology. There was also a quite nice girl, woman rather, who had once been Miss America, or it may have been several girls, serially, who had once been, in different years, Miss America. Dear Ed was still trying to get Beard laid, but Beard could not enter the situation cold, not just like that. Then there was a big party at Ed's bungalow mansion in Bel Air, and it was now that everything began to change and seeds of as yet unvoiced and unrealized doubt at the viability of phrases like *death is crap* started, silent and sparse and invisible and widespread, to be scattered. For now Paola emerged from the press of crown-teethed agents, directors, musical arrangers, actors and the rest. She was introduced to him as Paula Lucretia Belly, so that he did not first take her for Italian. If a man could have a name like Schaumwein, Belly was not impossible even for a slender girl like this. But she turned out to be Paola Lucrezia Belli, a surname meaning, Beard supposed, *of the family of beautiful ones*, appropriate enough for this member of it. That final vowel had to be well lifted. She spoke English well with British sounds but Mediterranean *bel canto*. She asked him first about his own name.

'To be called Beard and not to have a beard is strange or perhaps it is not strange. But it is a thing that must be remarked on often to you.'

'In the army mostly. *Living up to your name, Beard* was what they said on parade. But of course I always shaved very carefully, knowing it would be said. The fact is that I do have rather a heavy beard. I have to shave twice a day. But I've never grown a real beard, no. That would be wrong somehow, I think.'

She listened to all this with polite care. She said then: 'I first met your name in the Pasquino cinema in Rome. In Trastevere. They show films in English there. You had written the *sceneggiatura* for a film I saw that I liked. An Anglo-French-German film. With an Italian director.'

'*The Doomsday Girl?*' Beard said. 'Oh, but they changed so much. He did, I mean, Ruffini. All directors want to write, but all they can do is rewrite. It didn't end at all the way I wrote it.'

'The bones of it were good,' she said, in the somewhat deep voice that seemed at first to assort ill with her small compact body, especially when so many of these superb Californian giantesses dealt in squeaks. 'It had good bones.' She looked down from his eyes as though to examine his own bones, hidden behind one of his Brunei lightweight suits, and then up to his eyes again, which were about ten inches higher than hers. Her eyes were large, clear and wide-spaced, candy-coloured with gold sprinklings; the black eyebrows arched somewhat high; a lot of black Mediterranean hair tumbled in a carefully careless cloud on to her low white brow.

'You're in er movies?' he asked.

'A photographer,' she said. 'Still photographs for magazines. I was today photographing Frank Sinatra at his rehearsals.' There was, on the Warner Brothers estate, a building that housed this entertainer's Enterprises, not far from the castle that had been raised for *Camelot*.

'Was he very rude to you?' She seemed about thirty, perhaps younger. She was informally dressed in sweater and micro-skirt and boots.

'I do not notice. I am just a camera darting about. You cannot be rude to a camera.'

'You speak English well. *Darting about* – very idiomatic. Where did you learn it?'

'My husband was from Trinidad. Now we are divorced.'

An announcement of marital status, as the official forms put it. 'I,' Beard said, 'am a widower.'

'This I know,' she said. 'Ed said about it.' She gave him a look of a kind he would have called, in a script, appraising, as though Ed had discussed with her, though this seemed unlikely, the need for Beard to be laid and her own suitability for the duty of laying. Then, in the loud and cheerful commerce of the party, Beard became separated from her. He went to one of the bathrooms, where the toilet was at first hard to find, being covered with a mink rug, and there appraised, since he had just evoked the term, himself in the mirror. Fifty, yes: it was in the eye-lines and the slight sag of the chin. But it was an acceptable face, surely, especially with Californian sunflush, and the teeth were a young man's. His dentist had once told him that he was one of the lucky few whose teeth would outlive him. He would have preferred his work to, but you could not have everything. He had no paunch, only a gentle Silenus-as-a-boy swelling. Both face and body had good bones. The time had then come seriously, or perhaps not too much so, to think about being laid, laying rather. Not specifically this Miss or Signorina Belli, but it was the sense that she was real, solid, probably undepilated, probably also garlic-smelling if one got close enough, and not glamorously vacuous like the California goddesses who gloried in belonging to the two-dimensional culture that smelt of nothing, that was beginning to indicate to him that the frivolity had to be taken out of this laying business. It was to do, he saw, with his being a European, however peripheral a one. Forget about laying and think more of making love. But *love* too might be the wrong word, since love was what had subsisted between Leonora and himself, or so they had said to each other nearly every other day. *Amore*, perhaps, was the right word.

At the end of the party Beard discovered that he and Paola Lucrezia Belli were both staying at the Beverly-Wilshire and that a certain Chuck Megroz, who trade was that of studio orchestral harpist, was going in that direction and more than willing to drive them thither. Beard and Paola sat together in the back of the giant vehicle, which gave out Debussy's *Sacred and Profane Dances* stereophonically as they travelled, and he wondered whether he should hold her hand, a small brownish capable-looking one. Instead he contented himself with humming *La ci darem la mano*, despite the Debussy, and she responded, also humming, with *Vorrei e non vorrei*. That meant nothing.

They found their rooms were on the same floor, but she was quick to *dar* him her *mano* in a conventional good-night shake and then, head high in a fine Italian posture, stride off. So he shambled off, found he could not sleep, being obscurely excited, and worked in bed on a lyric for *The Lovers of the Lake*, tentative title. When giggly nonsense like 'Mary Shelley sees/ Hairy-bellied bees'/ began, to the tune of 'Honeysuckle Rose', to smoke into his consciousness, he knew he was ready to yield it to sleep. But 'Belli' and 'belly' lingered; he wondered why, with the example of the Song which is Solomon's so shining, 'belly' had become comic or offensive in demotic speech. The air is flowery with flowers. The sky is belly with bells. He slept. He did not dream.

The telephone woke him at seven-ten. He answered it, but

20

there was no one there, strange. Two minutes later there was a knock, strange, and he went to the door, naked except for a bath-towel, having no night clothes now, travelling light from the first of spring on, and found Paola there, barefooted, blue-quilted, hair loose. He let her in at once, saying, 'Was it you who rang just now?'

'It was to wake you,' she said, letting her dressing-gown fall to the carpet (as some girl had done in a television play he'd written) and (but not like that girl because of the need to purvey Good Family Viewing) getting into bed wonderfully and totally naked.

'And was this, did this,' said, grabbing his battery shaver and shearing off his night's beard, Beard, trembling, leaving patches. 'Ed, I mean, did Ed? I have to do this, sorry, I'm like a matchbox first thing in the —'

'First thing in the morning is always better than night. No, it's me, not he. You looked lost, also nice. Hurry.'

'And please,' he said, asperging aftershave, 'it's been such a long time. Don't laugh at me, don't.'

'It is allowed to smile though?' she smiled. He was in there with her, as totally if not so wonderfully naked. He had her in his arms, flooding with relief, gratitude, lust, affection, anger at so long a deprivation, guilt inevitably at having rejected (for that was what the companionate marriage had been chiefly about) Leonora's gross sick body, now very sharply presented to him in terms of this lissom healthy one. Her kiss tasted of toothpaste and wallfruit, one tracing of her warm back's curve gently down to the waist and more opulently out to the buttocks made him wish to sob with a complex emotion that seemed closer to a kind of cosmic rage than the humility of thankfulness at a bliss so long denied now to be so openly granted. Anyway, it was a bliss prolonged ending in many kisses, for which he had not realized how hungry he was, and this meant words that were their corollaries, like 'my love' and *amore*, 'darling' and *tesoro mio*. At eight-thirty there was a knock and then the sound of the door opening. 'Breakfast,' Beard said. 'I always hang the order up the night before. There'll be enough for two.'

The brown waiter wheeled it in – orange juice, coffee, cereal, cream, fried eggs, corned beef hash, ham, yoghurt, a bread basket, a clinking pitcher of iced water. She watched from beneath the bedclothes; he was up, towel round him, to sign the bill. The towel slid off as he signed. She laughed. He said to both: 'Sorry about that.' The waiter said, in good, even professorial, English:

'The natural condition of humanity. No occasion for regret. Enjoy your breakfast.'

Her mouth flecked with yoghurt, chewing on a croissant dipped in black coffee, she said: 'Do you always eat so big a breakfast?'

'Only when Warner Brother are paying. Besides, I don't need lunch after this lot, and lunch always makes me sleepy.' He offered her two fried eggs. She shook her hair. She grasped him impulsively by his wristwatch and sprayed crumbs on his forearm, saying:

'I must be quick. I have to photograph somebody –'

'Who?' he asked jealously. 'Bloody Sinatra again?'

'A striptease artist who has now become a great actress. She was in *The Gun of Love* I think it is named. And then my plane is at eleven-thirty. To Rome.'

So this was what it had all been leading to. 'Trastevere?'

'How did you know? Yes, Piazza Santa Cecilia.'

'No,' he said in pain. And then in loud agony, the forkful of corned beef hash crashing to his plate, 'No, no, no, you can't, you mustn't.'

'I can and I must. I have my work.'

'You don't have to have it, I'll work for both of us. I'll be getting fifty thousand dollars for this script, less agent's commission, God curse him.' And then: 'I'm coming with you.' Then: 'I can't. Not today. I have to see this man Flesher or

22

Fleischer or Fisher. To talk about songs. But tomorrow, **yes**. Or the next day.'

'I go from Rome to Paris the next day. Then I am back in Rome next week.'

'I can't let you go, I can't.' He pushed the corned beef hash aside and, bath-towel dropping from him again, tried to take her in his arms. She pushed him off and pulled her dressing-gown to modest tightness at the neck. He said, his heart sinking and thumping: 'I'll be in Rome, I'll be there.'

She appraised him gravely and then leaned over and gave him a good full affectionate kiss. 'I like to kiss you,' she said. 'I have not liked to kiss many men.' The California sun ripped through the smog and irradiated the ruined breakfast table.

Two

'But what is there in it of a narrative?' she asked, having kissed his left shoulder. 'I mean, what in it makes a good film?' They were in bed together at nine-fifteen of a bright Trastevere morning.

'I have to have Byron trying to make violent love to Mary Shelley and then Percy Shelley striking out at him but not standing a chance, Byron being a boxer and swimmer and cricketer. And Lady Caroline Lamb arrives, dressed as a boy, all in velvet. Shelley falls for her and Mary goes angrily off to write *Frankenstein*. There's a lot going on really. And of course there are the songs.'

She'd stopped listening after his first few words. 'What I must do,' she now said, 'is to photograph Rome not direct but – how would you say it?'

'Obliquely?'

'Yes. Rome in reflections. In rain water, you see. Or windows. I think we will have rain today. It is not quite the season for rain, but I think we will have it.'

'So we stay in bed then and wait for the rain?' He smiled lovingly and grasped her boldly. He had lost much of his timidity in three weeks and had ceased to talk of the gap in their ages, less wide than he had originally believed, for he now knew she was thirty-three. But a new cause for timidity, or perhaps for triumph, had recently come about: the husband from whom she was divorced was a greater man than he – no mere script-writer but a genuine novelist and one he had read and partially admired – P. R. Pathan, author of *Hell Is a City* and *A Remoter World* and *Her False Mouth*, all much-praised novels, and *My Dungeon or My Grave*, a work of premature autobiography. He was, as he knew from Who's Who as well as from her reluctant lips, for she no longer wished to talk about him, thirty-eight years old with a lifetime of moderate fame in front of him. Who's Who had no entry for Beard, Ronald; Beard would only know fame vicariously. Still, Pathan, despite his Caribbean-Aryan beauty, brown body, brains, had been a bad husband, drunk, cruel, loud, impotent. 'Poor sweetheart,' he said, kissing her. She pushed him away; she had had enough love for one morning.

'Why poor?'

'You need coffee, I've been cruel, I haven't got up and made you coffee.' And he got up now to make it, pulling on old trousers and a shirt and sports coat, working garb. The kitchen was small and full of dirty dishes: this delicious and loved Italian girl had no gift of Welsh tidiness, but to hell with that, death being the ultimate tidiness. He charged and put on the gas-flame the heavy Italian coffee-pot and then went into the living-room to look out of the window. The snow-stoned *putti* on the façade of the basilica opposite writhed fatly in the sun; the little square was full of parked cars; a man outside his shop was making or repairing or something iron bedsteads with a loud blowtorch. Vehicles were loudly petulant filing through the narrow street, *senso unico*, to his right. A fat man in a garage over to his left sang '*Domani non ci sono, domani vado via.*' Well, so, the coins in Trevi had worked their magic and brought him back. Clouds swallowed the sun; she was right about there going to be rain.

He poured a cup of black bitter coffee and took it to her in bed. She was looking critically at proofs of some of her photographs: she did not do the laboratory work herself; it was done somewhere round the corner here, at the back of the restaurant called Da Meo Patacca. This was mainly an open-air restaurant, very loud at night with singers and a squad of trumpeters who played 'The Stars and Stripes Forever'. The photographs she was looking at were of members of the Italian government that had recently fallen, leering men not to be trusted and in consequence untrusted. 'Darling,' he said. The floor by her bedside was littered with sundered pages of *Paesa Sera* and *Il Messaggero* and *Corriere della Sera*, also magazines like *L'Espresso* and *Panorama* and *Il Mondo*. She reserved order to her art. '*Tesoro*,' she said, taking the coffee. He drank coffee with her, well diluted with milk. He would have preferred tea, but they were out of tea-bags; they were also now out of milk; indeed, they were out of most things except pasta and canned tomatoes. But they would lunch at the Rugantino, probably, and dine at – they would think of that when they came to it.

She had to go out and see somebody that morning, some rogue at a newspaper office who had still not paid her for a photograph they had printed a month before, and play Italian hell with him. He worked at his script distractedly, finished a scene in which Mary Shelley cried: 'We created him, we, this monster who tramples all Europe in the name of glory, this great trundling stone that crushes all in its path in the name of France . . .' Percy mumbled: '*Dieser Stein, dieser Frankenstein*.' No, that would not do, that was spelling it out too much. Beard tried a lyric for Percy: 'O wild west wind, where have you taken her?' That would not do either. But there was no urgency about getting it right; the thing to do was to ensure a sound structure, with good *bones*. He heard Paola saying the word and responded with a powerful burst of affection and desire. He went to the bedroom and lay on her part of the bed, prone, smelling the faintly burnt smell of her new-washed black hair on the pillow. Then, observing the crammed ashtrays, the wine glass with its purple dregs, the scattered paperbacks, the shallow tents of sundered *giornale* pages, the contagion of twenty-six years of tidy Welsh wife pushed him into thirty minutes of bringing order to all this. He reassembled the newspapers and piled them neatly with the magazines, made the bed and covered it with the big black fur rug, took the books into the living-room and stood them up on a shelf. There, he noticed for the first time, was a hardback of *A Remoter*

World, with P. R. Pathan, in a dust-cover portrait done by Jerry Bauer, being handsome and insolent. The title-page was scrawled with 'To my sweetest dearest most angelic love love and again love Prrrrrp.' So that had been his nickname, a kind of lip-fart acronym of his initials. Beard tore out the title-page and burnt it carefully in the metal waste-basket. Then he opened the book at random and read:

'. . . her nipples ironhard and boring through his chest as he mounted her body, which was all fire. In his nostrils was the burnt odour of her newly washed black hair. He could not wait any longer, entering her at once, his own iron hardness welcomed and gulped by her soft eager openness, moist to brimming. Open mouth clamped on open mouth, then sundered, she breathing fast and harsh to the sky, he with a kind of snoring desperation into the folds of the raincoat that was their pillow. He could not hold back, he could not, nor did she wish him to, gasping *yes yes* into his ear. When he came, it was like the bursting in the fire of a keg of honey, her cry of affirmation became a long high note of fulfilment, they lay then, spent, gasping, thankful, while the little sounds of the outer world began slowly to impinge . . .'

Well, he had to write that sort of thing, being a well-regarded novelist. He, Beard, like Virgil, must be content with the barest appeals to remembered adult experience – '*nota flamma*' or '21. INT DAY HIS BEDROOM They lie on the bed and make love.' Novelists were not, of course, gentlemen. P. R. Pathan was a swine. Beard looked for other of Pathan's books and found a paperback of *My Dungeon or My Grave*. He stuffed both works into the kitchen garbage-can. Then he went back to the spare room she called *lo studio* and tried once more, though now it seemed impossible, to work. Work had been easy a year, or less, ago, without physical desire raging around like a ham actor. Now there was jealousy, an emotional complex of awesome obtuseness. The Pathan business was all over, wasn't it? Yes, but its being all over meant that it once existed. For God's sake, be reasonable. Jealousy opened its thick lips at

27

that, dribbling, not knowing the word. And now Shelley, in-effectual angel, looked reproachfully at Beard, burbling about the love of pure minds. *I've already had that*, Beard growled, for all the world like jealousy itself; *now I want a bit of body.*

He was in the bathroom masturbating when the noonday gun thudded from the Gianicolo and the Angelus started clanging from several campaniles. You were allowed to masturbate in the absence of the beloved: he had read that in Havelock Ellis or some other great sexological primitive. Beard did not doubt that Shelley had masturbated, in spite of all his fine talk. Byron? Probably not; probably no time. Beard checked his fly before leaving the apartment. He was to meet Paola in the Rugantino at one or thereabouts; but he wished first to find something reasonable in the panatela line, Italy being no paradise for the smoker of brown things, several shops having to be visited before even the humblest cigar need could be met. It was lucky for him that he heard the rain start to finger-drum on the dove-stained glass dome that lidded the stairwell at the very moment of his opening the apartment door. This meant he could go straight back in and put on his white raincoat. If the rain had begun when he had completed the long descent and was preparing to leave the building, he would have seen it as a heart-failing task to climb up again. It was a hell of a climb, no doubt about it. So he would have had to get very wet.

There was a letter for him, c/o Belli, in the rusted wall-box below. It was from a film-composer named Trenchmore, to whom he had let the Hammersmith house. There would be trouble with the neighbours, for Trenchmore could not compose film music out of his head; he had to bang about on his Steinway grand, looking for themes and discords. The letter indeed said something about the neighbours banging on the wall, but Trenchmore banged back on the piano louder, so everything seemed to be all right. The gas water-heater was not working too well and the television was on the blink, but everything otherwise was all right. Maisie sent her love and the kids were all right. They envied him in sunny Rome there, raining like buggery every day here in Hammersmith. *Chow*, or whatever the valediction was.

'*Ciao*,' Beard said in greeting to a small child coming in soaked with a packet of butterfly pasta and beginning to climb the stairs. The child did not respond. At the corner tobacconist's Beard had to wait while a very old woman, who had been hearing about an impending salt shortage, bought three kilos of salt. He was glad to see on the shelves a new consignment of the Belgian panatelas called Mercator: a tolerable smoke. He bought five packets and walked on towards the Viale di Trastevere, smiling to himself in the rain as he thought of Paola, in her element like a duck. No, not like a duck, not at all like a duck. She would be clicking away at Rome reflected in puddles. She was unclear about the aesthetic, even the commercial, motivation for this obliquity of view. Something unusual, perhaps make up a book with captions he, Beard, could provide. A sort of ghost look at Rome.

Oh, no. Oh Christ, no. God, keep ghosts out of it. He had had a dream last night about his first wife alive again and saying *darling here I am, did you miss me?* In the dream Paola was in his life but not in the house, wherever it was, not one he recognized, and he faced the horror of telling Leonora that he'd understood she was dead, had made a new start, loved someone else. There the dream ended. He hurried shuddering on to the Viale, which was an incubus of traffic, the drivers operatic on their horns, and crossed with others, safety in numbers, he seeking the newspaper stall near the Garibaldi bridge. Today's *Times* might already be in. He noted again how much Italian girls had changed in the last few years – longer-legged, not at all ducklike, positively American. When he got to the newspaper stall, just opposite the Reale cinema, he found the only English language paper there was the *Daily American*, published in Rome for Roman Americans. Well, one could not expect a British paper for Roman Britons, such no longer existing since the departure of the legions. The British hardly at all existed for Europe, except as a Common Market abstration, as fish and chip and beer consumers on the Costa del Sol, as football rowdies. He, Beard, was usually taken for either an American or a German. Good Christ, things had been different in the days of the lovers of Leman.

Beard looked across at the top-hatted and frock-coated statue of the Roman dialect poet Belli, to whose family Paola claimed to belong. That man had been thoroughly nonconformist and had written a large number of blasphemous sonnets. There was one, for instance, on the foreskin of Jesus Christ which, in Belli's day, had been on simultaneous exhibition in over eighty Catholic churches. God, the poet suggested, had enabled this foreskin to grow like a fingernail, so that portions could be clipped off *per omnia saecula saeculorum* to edify the faithful. Beard had determined to read and understand a Belli sonnet every day, with Paola's help, perhaps later to translate and publish, in some arty bold journal of America, twenty or more of the more obscene sonnets, so that he could be more than a mere script-maker. Also it would be good for his Roman, if not for his Italian. Belli was all right, both Bellis were all right. He smiled again, recrossing the Viale in some danger, passed the Esperia cinema – lower-class, cheaper and noisier than the Reale – and arrived at the Rugantino.

He liked the Rugantino, which had a what he thought of as Northern quality, meaning, in his rough and uninstructed regional mythology, not at all Neapolitan. Tablecloths were clean, waiters quick, oil and garlic subdued, Anita Ekberg had once danced on a table in profound décolletage, Jean-Paul Sartre and Simone de Beauvoir had shared something bland and left their autographs. Beard sat at a small table and ordered gin and tonic. He also read part of the *Daily American*. The major item of news concerned war in the Middle East, which had just broken out again, and it was illustrated with a grinning photograph of patch-eyed General Moshe Dayan, newly appointed Defence Minister of Israel. Beard moved on to the cartoon page and read 'Dear Abby': human problems, daughter unrepentant at being in unmarried family way, my brother-in-law has a habit of scratching his groin that turns me on. Beard was not greatly interested in other people's wars; he had a six-year one of his own. Nor did he consider that peace, as it was called, was necessarily a desirable thing. War, someone had written, was a mode of cultural transmission. If, said dear Abby, her husband had started pinning up beefcake cutouts in the bathroom, this did not necessarily mean that he was turning into a fag. Some men's temperaments were highly complex.

'*Tesoro mio,*' she said, 'good news.' She had come in, straight out of a taxi, wearing a kind of Chinese worker's outfit he was sure she had not left the flat in; she had left the flat in something much more decadent, showing a lot of leg. Ducklike, indeed. He frowned: she reminded him of somebody. She put down a bag labelled *Upim*. Had bought this then, tried on, stayed with it. 'I am going to Israel,' she said happily, sitting down with her two cameras still about her neck, beaming at the beaming waiters.

'What? Why? Who says you're going to?'

'You have a *giornale*,' she said. 'Look, it is war. Israel and the Arabs. Vincenzo Bonicelli is being sent out to cover it, I am to do the pictures. Isn't it good news?'

'No, it is not good news. You'll be shot at. You'll be killed. You're not going.' Peace then was, after all, a desirable thing. 'You can't go, not now when you and I –'

'It won't be a long war, they say at the *Mondiale* –'

'They're sending you, are they? Swine, *farabutti*. You're not going, I won't let you go.'

'We go this evening, there is a plane to Tel Aviv this evening.'

'But you're supposed to be here, doing these pictures of Rome.' He had no authority over her, of course, love conferring no authority, marriage was a different thing altogether. 'We ought to be married,' he said. 'I told you in London we ought to be married.' For she had been in London taking hippic pictures of Princess Anne, they had gone over together for a

31

couple of days, he arranging about the letting of the house and begging his bank for lire.

'This morning I did forty pictures. The rain has stopped, see, but the puddles are still there, so I can do forty more in the afternoon.'

'This afternoon,' he said firmly, 'we have other things to do.' She put her small hand on his. And then he said: 'What the hell am I thinking about? If you go I'm going with you.'

'You stay here,' she said. 'I want to know that you're safe, here, in Rome.' That was love, that sounded like love. 'And to collect the proofs of the pictures and to start thinking how we can make a book.' She began to read the menu avidly. The waiter waited, an Italian film-star type with lustrous sideburns. '*Zuppa di verdura,*' she ordered. '*Uova stracciate al formaggio.*' Beard said: 'For me, very little. I have no appetite. Cold beef and gherkins.' She said: 'And a bottle of Lambrusco di Sorbara. We must celebrate.'

And then, when the waiter had gone, 'Marriage,' she said. 'It is no good talking of marriage. Outside Italy I am divorced, but here in Italy not. The divorce is not recognized in Italy.'

'We can leave Italy then, damn it. We can be married in England, as I said when we were there. We could live in England. There are lots of advantages to living in England.' Such as? Well, pubs perhaps. The superior quality of the television programmes. He couldn't, to be honest, think of anything else. She said:

'I have to be in Italy. I have to fight the government. Also the Vatican.' It seemed a large assignment for so small, though not excessively fragile, a girl. 'Both are there for crushing women. Marriage too is for crushing women.'

'Not with me,' he said. 'There'd be no crushing with me. Damn it, you've had a fair sample of what it would be like. Marriage with me, that is. I even tidied up this morning. Made the bed.'

'There was no need to do that,' she said. 'Life is not the making of beds but the unmaking of beds.' That sounded like a quotation, but from whom? Not Dante, certainly. Moravia? Pirandello? It would have been ungracious to ask, as she smiled with radiant meaningfulness, saying it, and squeezed his hand. Ariosto, probably.

But, when they had drained the Lambrusco and their thimbles of espresso, the way to bed proved circuitous. Forty more in the afternoon, she had said, meaning now. So she clicked away at reflections, in glass doors and windows as well as puddles, very intent, but ready, when reloading, to be radiant at the prospect of flying out to be shot at by Arabs or Jews or both. But then, in the Piazzi di Santa Maria in Trastevere, she saw someone she knew coming out of a restaurant. 'No,' she said with fear. '*Porco Giuda.*' It was a tall black girl, gliding like a queen or a model, the sort, or perhaps the very girl, symbolizing for Federico Fellini the ultimate in the glamour of the great world, golden deprovincializer of shoddy Rome or Venice or Florence. She was with a fat waddling man, perhaps a producer. 'What's the matter, darling?' said Beard.

'She's back,' said Paola, huge-eyed in distress. 'That means he may be back too.'

'Who?' He knew who. 'Prrrp?' So this then was the fellow-coloured Paola had told him Pathan was now shacked up with. Glamour, all right, loads of it, high-breasted, scarlet-swathed, striding from the hip and each stride an alexandrine jewelled with superbity. The hair too piled high with insolence.

'They were supposed to be in New York,' Paola said. 'I read that he was a professor in New York.' Beard looked kindly at the paunched Romans agape at the black glamour. She strode in cosmopolitan insolence, high and svelte, towards Via di Santa Maria della Scala, her fat companion awaddle after. Beard said:

'Perhaps that one there left him, whoever she is.'

'Gimpy. Her name's Gimpy.'

It was hard somehow to see this Gimpy as the consort of a professor, even in New York. Another thing: dirty novelists became professors, script-writers didn't. 'After all,' Beard said, 'he's impotent and a real bastard and so forth.' But Paola's eyes were greatly full of cloudy Rome and foreboding. She said:

'Be careful when I'm away. Do not open the door. Not to anyone.'

'You mean that bastard might come round? What would he come round for?'

'He's a savage man. He might even have a gun.'

'Look,' Beard said. 'Filthy impotent West Indian novelists don't scare me, gun or no gun. But I still don't see what he'd want to come round for.'

'He wants things. Things I have he says are not mine. He wrote letters. And then there were letters from an *avvocato*. I did not answer. It is all really revenge.' Beard nodded. That word made more sense in warm Italy, though wet, than in cold England, also and more wet. A brown novelist with a gun, teeth agleam, wanting his revenge. But then:

'What revenge? Why? I thought it was he who'd done all the wrong. It's you who ought to have the revenge.'

'Oh, stupid,' she said. 'His mind does not work in a normal way.' In a dirty novelist's way, then, call it that. He said no more. In the South they took vendettas and honour and things far too seriously. Her teeth clenching her lower lip, she encased her working camera and led the way home.

She was at first in no mood for the making of love. There was the question of packing a kind of soldier's haversack which was hiding under the bed, as though having long awaited patiently a fratricidal Semite war. No nonsense, nothing frilly, no exposing of limbs or bosoms to desert tanks and the crack of rifles. Beard sat on the made bed and watched her, weary after the lunch, the picture-taking circuit and, above all, the damnable climb to the top of the apartment building. Those stairs could well be the death of him. Death on such stairs could also well come for a cardiac character in one of his scripts, and the character could well, in the 'setting up' process, feel about those stairs as he, Beard, felt about these. Resigned to her leaving, he now began to fuss about her departure time, reporting time, getting a taxi to take them both to the airport, for he must see her off to the wars. 'Vincenzo will come for me in his car,' she said, packing one more brassière and an Italian-Hebrew phrasebook she had bought that morning. 'He will also bring the tickets. He is never late. Don't worry.'

'But I'm to see you off?'

'No. I don't like it. There is nothing to say but the same things again and again. You will stay here. *Amore*.' Then she embraced him. Clasping her on the bed in her Chinese worker's outfit, he caught an abrupt physical memory of the girl he had, he had thought and still thought, been in love with. So that was the one. Had she been Paola's precursor? Or would Paola seem some day, and perhaps soon, to be a belated effort at recalling that girl's crisp black hair, muskiness, compact and ready flesh? Her name had been Miriam, she had had a married sister in Israel, and he had first embraced her when she had been clad as a sergeant of the British auxiliary army. He had then recently become a civilian, and there was a mild piquancy in the contrast of the new, feminine-seeming, softness of his clothes with the rough serge of hers. But, when her clothes were off, the excitement her body aroused was the greater for the lack of allure of the stiff discarded carapace. It had been, like this, a Mediterranean body, savoured the more because of the diet of Northern blondness he had, on a month's demobilization leave, consumed almost to surfeit in Leonora's bed. It had been a time of mutual infidelity, to be expected after a long war. And then there had been mutual remorse and wholesome resolves, and fidelity had been resumed – wholly on his part, more or less on hers. But the passion for Miriam had not been able, through an excess of indulging it, ever to decline; it had not even approached the limit of appetite when they kissed good-bye. He had never let it become a nostalgia of the senses: he had filed it away as a grace and a wonder. The body Paola now disclosed was not that one, the pleasures it gave were other and maturer; but, through an accident of the feel of cloth, it warmed of physical nostalgia. Dangerous to revive that past which contained a young and comely Leonora; he wanted to live in the future. But the fierceness of the love he made now was, in a manner, that of the man twenty years younger who had lain with Miriam. It was, God help him, the best love they had made. She said:

'Too good. Dangerously good.'

'You mean, I hope, that you've changed your mind about going to Israel?'

'No, *stupido*. Life is not so simple. And that is the danger, that life is not so simple. There are some things you do and — I cannot explain easily, not even in Italian. Like to disturb things. To indent the natural order. Like magic.'

'Dangerous?' He lay back. 'That's a good phrase — *indent the natural order*.'

'To invoke,' she said, lighting a tipped Dunhill. And then, looking at her watch, '*Dio mio*, the time. Listen, I don't know yet where I'll be in Tel Aviv. I'll try to telephone, but it's never easy to telephone Rome from abroad. And after Tel Aviv I don't know where I'll be. I'll be where the war is.'

'No, no,' he cried, clasping her again. She pushed him away, getting up, and said:

'Take those rolls of film tomorrow, you know where.'

'What do you mean,' watching her dress in her uniform, a kind of olive-colour, '*invoke?*'

'They should have them ready the following day. Watch out for that man. Don't open the door to anyone.'

'Darling, darling.'

'Get on with your work while I'm away. Try to learn some Italian.'

'I'm learning some Roman. Belli, I mean. Angel, don't go.' And then: 'Invoke what?'

'I don't know, I haven't time to think of it. I'm hungry.'

'But you had a large lunch. And there'll be something to eat on the plane.'

'I'm hungry.'

He sighed and went naked into the kitchen. The only thing

he could give her was spaghetti and tomato sauce. Tomorrow and the days after that he faced the problem of shopping in Italian. 'This spaghetti isn't quite ready yet.' She looked at the pasta writhing in the boiling water. She said:

'In two minutes they'll be ready. *Spaghetti* is plural, you can't say *spaghetti* is.'

'In English you can and must.'

Stirring the sauce, he winced as some splashed on to his midriff. She licked it off like blood. 'Spaghetti *are*.'

'*Is*.' He embraced her an instant, he naked, she dressed like a soldier. 'I must put something on,' he said, 'down here, any-way.' She tried a forkful of spaghetti, nodding hot-mouthed that they were done, then festooned his rod with a few white strands, like a maypole. 'Ow ow.' He went to dress.

While she was eating, they heard a honking below and the crying of her name. He went to the window to see a squat handsome Roman standing by a silver-grey Mercedes, flashing his teeth up through the damp air. He waved down. 'So,' he said, 'this is it. Have you got everything? God, your passport.' It was in a drawer and had the name Paola Lucrezia Pathan. He nodded sadly. A quick embrace and she was out of the apartment. He leaned out again, watching for her to emerge into the piazza. The lamps were coming on, each doubled in the still wet cobbles. There she was: a kiss on the cheek for the toothy Roman, a wave upward, into the car, off to Fiumi-cino. How did he know she existed? There was the plate of spaghetti-ends and sauce; her cigarette butts lay, fumed to the limit, in the ashtrays. Clothes in the drawers and the one ward-robe. Shoes. Books. No, she existed because she was sewn into his ears, lips, skin. Her absence denoted existence enough.

His aloneness was the more intense now because he was surrounded by an alien culture and police force. He went into *lo studio* where Byron and the Shelleys were waiting, people of his own blood, practitioners of a trade not wholly incognate with his own, but they looked coldly up at him, forced as they were into the postures of a ridiculous song. Besides, they knew all about Italy and Italians, proud exiles. Shelley had even written an Italian lyric called *Buona Notte* which Beard had thought of using. He glumly turned off the *studio* light and bit his thumb-nail in the corridor. He would eat something British this evening, shopping in Italian starting earlier than expected, and the stairs would near kill him a second time this day. But bravely he went down to the lighted shops. The general store next to the tobacconist was full of corseted women fluting arias of lament. '*Si, dottore?*' said the shopman, insincerely radiant. Beard bought a *scatola* of corned beef from Israel, he presumed it was, and a *scatola* of condensed milk, also *bustine* of tea. Then he went to the greengrocer and bought a kilo of *patate* and what the hell were onions called *cipolle*. He climbed desperately wheezing back up, unlocked gasping, then lay on the corridor floor awhile. When breath had sufficiently returned, he cooked himself the Liverpool dish, also served in Cardiff, known as lobscouse.

Communication. He wondered about communication as, feeling British robustness return with the strong sweet tea, he watched an American western on the tiny television set. '*Ciao, ragazzi,*' Gary Cooper said, swinging into the saloon. A thug called Chuck delivered an insulting speech in what seemed to be the Piedmontese dialect. Beard switched off and went to lie on the bed. The coarse warbling of *Arrivederci Roma* came up from Da Meo Patacca, also American voices of delight at being in Italy. He was not in a state of sexual excitement and could think more or less coldly, telling himself that the end of a marriage, whether through the death of life or of love, was also the end of a civilization. More than twenty-six years spent in constructing a mythology, a joint memory-bank, a language, a signalling system of grunt and touch – all gone, wasted. Perhaps so closed, even incestuous, a semiotic complex had to exclude the international language of sex, sneering that – as Esperanto and Volapük showed – an international language was no language at all. But when a civilization died, it became as evil as rotted meat, and he had to find his good now in an international language. Or could a new civilization be built? The obstacles were staggering.

It would take him a long time, for instance, to understand how an Italian woman felt about Italy. A child under Mussolini, a pubescent girl when the war ended in chaos and corruption and military lechery, Paola had become a woman in a bad culture whose cynicism was only redeemed by the grosser Catholic tenets, which seemed to mean chiefly keeping women low. Marriage sacred, but male adultery condoned. Religion perhaps to be regarded as having value only as a validant of *machismo*, or *gallismo* as they called it here. Certainly priest-hatred ran high, but perhaps only because a priest was neither a man nor a woman. This small girl in her pathetic Mao uniform had to fight the pasta-paunched leerers, the Holy Father, demagogues of the Christian Democrat party, the haranguers of all parties who extolled *lo spirito umano*, meaning men being fat-bellied and on top of women. No wonder she hated cooking and tidiness and the housewifely virtues and, yes, marriage itself. But she could do nothing about being beautiful and also amorous; she was stuck, as by original sin, with those attributes. Only in his arms would she yield to the closed world which the Vatican and the Questura and the politicians could not enter – not yet. That it had been the same closed world, and perhaps the same ecstasies, with Pathan and the others, whoever they had been, was to be discounted: solipsism was the word here, solipsism. As for his own ecstasies, he had, and was willing, to regard them as a more than fair exchange for the civilization that had been snuffed out with Leonora. He did not want even to remember it – evil, like chewing bad meat. It had been good for its time, but this was another time. No more nuances of speech, then, no codes, no shared culture of diet, jokes, memories, quotations. But magic, huge transports. Indentation of the natural order: a good phrase, hers. Invocation – what the hell did that mean?

He understood and got into bed with the draft script of the Leman story. Shelley, against a gorgeous Alpine panorama, burbled something again about the love of pure minds, straight out of *Epipsychididion*. 'Two angels in bed, holding hands,' so Mark Rampton had put it. And 'It would have been a good thing if that skylark had dropped a large white mess in Shelley's eye. Bird thou never wert, indeed. Blithe spirit, for God's sake.' Not Huxley's precise words, but to that effect. Beard remembered that he and Leonora had had a salve for any careless wound one gave to the other's self-esteem. An 'unpremeditated 'urt', they would call it. Try explaining that to Paola. 'Well, you see, *tesoro*, the last line of the Shelley stanza mentions *unpremeditated art*, and that's meant to rhyme with *wert*, do you see, do you see?' And, at a party, when Beard had been holding the floor too long with funny stories, Leonora would only have to say 'Mary' to stop him. That, *amore*, refers to Mr Bennet in *Pride and Prejudice* saying to his piano-playing daughter: 'Mary, you have delighted us long enough.' Do you see that?

No more. He recognized, with shock, a kind of disloyalty. But she ought to be here with him in bed, not in bloody Israel. Being away from him placed her in the same zone as Leonora and Miriam. Uniform, war, Israel, thy belly is as a mound of wheat. He stripped Sergeant Miriam Bloomfield of her uniform jacket, brass button by brass button, of her khaki tie and khaki shirt and regulation khaki brassière (you could, by God, see the War Department stamp on that warm hallowed binary nest) and embraced her naked upper body, aware of the rough W.D. skirt and lisle stockings and khaki knickers beneath – 'passion-crushers' the girls of the Auxiliary Territorial Service called them. They could not be more wrong. He crushed out the image – for Christ's sake no physical nostalgia but Paola should not have put on that bloody Chinese uniform – but could not crush out the hot spasm. Like a good scout after a serious chinwag from his scoutmaster, he escaped into sleep, leaving that most importunate dog to growl, shrug, then shrink into sleep with him. His lullaby was 'The Stars and Stripes Forever' played by the massed trumpets of Da Meo Patacca.

Three

Despite the continuing rain and the public fountains spewing surfeit, Rome had become suddenly niggardly with her domestic water. The following morning Beard lustrated against a lonely day by sitting in two cold inches and sopping with a logged sponge. He washed himself thoroughly nevertheless and, on an unbidden image of Saul Bellow the Canadian Jewish novelist for some reason frowning at him, paid special attention to his fundament. While on this he heard the telephone and slithered and fell towards it all soapy-arsed. Paola, it would be Paola's voice with gunfire behind it. It turned out to be a male voice, British and jaunty.

'Beard? Ron Beard?'

'Yes to both. Who?'

'This is Greg Greg. Here in the Infernal City.'

'Who? *Who?*'

'Come, come, boozer's memory, old man. Gregory Gregson. Brunei Town. You remember. Shawcross Importers Exporters.'

'Good God, you yes of course, well you, good God. How did you where did you. Damn, nearly slipped there, wet feet, just out of bath, marble floor, travertine really. I said where did you.'

'Well, leave in London and I rang your number and there was this woman's voice and a hell of a din, people banging on pianos and things, thought it couldn't be you, and they said you were here, so I thought to hell, break the journey back and —'

'You still there then? Good God.'

'The same firm, same foreign parts, old man. Selling Scotch and fridges in Kuching now, Sarawak.'

'Well, good God, old Greg, where are you now then?'

'Staying two nights at the Grand, come round and get pissed with your old pal, got in late last night, didn't ring, thought it was a bit late. I say, I was sorry to hear about –. She always seemed to me to be one of the best. Pity it had to happen.'

'Happens to us all sooner or later. I'm sorry too, well, you know. The Grand. I'll be round, see you in the bar then. Half an hour, say.'

'You do that one thing. Been quite a few years, still it'll be the same old Greg champing for a refill. Chow, or whatever it is they – Grand, bar, right, see you here then.' And the receiver went down.

So Beard was not to be lonely after all. He dressed for a high-class hotel, then put on his white raincoat. He remembered, first things first, that he had to remember to take Paola's films for developing and printing. He found the place among ancient stables, cursing all the while at the slippery cobbles, and it seemed to him that the two young men who ran it looked at him reproachfully. It was as if they knew he was going to get drunk in safe Rome while his beloved had to be shot at in Israel. *Domani*, they said. He went now to the statue of Belli, where there was a taxi-stand, but found no taxis because of the rain. He looked up in homage at the stone top hat, thinking of how the sestet of the sonnet on Judith and Holofernes might go in English:

> She held the head up in her lily hand,
>   Though it was heavy, horrible and gory,
> And did a tour of triumph through the land.
>   I find two morals in this holy story:
> A man can lose his head when fucking, and
>   A girl can be a whore for heaven's glory.

Polish it up a bit. Beard, translator of Belli, with the help of the other Belli. He saw a memory of a painting of that decapitation – whose? Caravaggio's – and the face of Judith was the face of Paola. Or was it the face of Miriam? He had, he feared, no real memory for faces. A taxi crawled in, and he took it to the smart international zone of the Via Veneto. Americans walked in gloom and with blind cameras, fed up with the rain.

It was early for Roman drinking, but Gregory Gregson was at it in the empty bar. He was, of course, fatter, shinier, balder. 'Hm,' he said, after greeting pummelling,' you don't look bad on it, not bad at all.'

'On what? Gin and tonic, large, large gin that is, small tonic.'

'On gay bachelorhood. Mustn't call it *gay* now though, must we? *Gay* means being a bloody pouf.'

'Mustn't call it bachelorhood. How's your little – Forgotten her name. Probably a different one now, though.'

'Aminah? It's Aminah's daughter, strangely enough or not so. Aminah went off with Parkinson, you remember Parkinson? Isa's her name, the daughter that is, only fifteen or so she says but you can't believe any of them. It's the name worries me, it means Jesus of course. Safe in the arms of Jesus. Jesus loves me, not that she does, bitch. What's this I hear about you taking up with an Eyetie bint? Ah.' The drinks came. '*Selamat minum.*'

'*Salute.*' Gregson's suit was clearly revealed, now Beard was used to the dim light, as tropical worsted, as though he had already left Western civilization behind, wog and wop being much of a muchness. 'Eyetie bint,' Beard repeated coldly. 'I don't actually think of her as an Eyetie bint.'

'Ah, like that, is it?' He sang quite loudly, as if as an earnest of what he would do later when properly fried: '*When the moon hits your eye like a big piece of pie, that's amoray.*' He seemed both to raise his glass to Beard's ménage and to thrust the glass like a glass phallus. 'Got a picture of her?' he wink-leered.

'Well, no.' No, he hadn't. He should have, but he hadn't. She took pictures, she didn't have pictures taken. 'She's – well –'

'Like Gina or Sophia or Claudia whatshername? Slow, old man, out of practice, dreadful thing. Come on.' And to the waiter: 'Similar, John. Oh, swill-a da glasses with a kichey drop of *merah*, right? Angostura to you.' To Beard, seriously: 'Still carrying on a bit, was she? A bit once too often. There comes a limit. Well, you must have known. Always did, you know, you must have known she did.'

'Who? Leonora? Carrying on? No, it was a pretty quiet sort of life. Yes, I did know. With you too, I should think. I can say that now it's all over.'

'Well.' Gregson ran a finger smartly along his thin grey moustache, very accurately, so that one could not think he was wiping his nose. 'It was the way things were out there, you know that. I always say a white woman should never go to the tropics. Good thing the Empire's over in a way. Sake of the wives. Who was it said that the loss of India would be the fault of the memsahibs? Said it damn near a hundred years ago, a sort of a prophet. Kipling? *By the old Moulmein pagoda, looking lazy at the sea.*' He did not sing the line too loud.

'She won't do it again,' Beard said. The new gins were pinkish. 'Cheers.'

'*Selamat.* Well, they get past it, you know. How old would she be now? Middle forties?'

'That's a queer sort of way of asking a – Like that damn poem of Daddy Wordsworth's, "We Are Seven" or something. What do you mean, how old would she –'

'She looked all right to me, very smart. Day before I phoned. Didn't think to before, thought you'd probably gone off somewhere else, very hard to stand more than six months of U.K. after being out East. So I thought, and looked you up in the book, and lo and behold – Well, I was right in a way, wasn't I, about you I mean. You here, that is, what is hardly U.K. by a long chalk. Of course, I didn't think for one moment –'

Beard gaped through all this. Then he said: 'You saw her? Where did you see her?'

'I'd just come out of the Playboy Club with a man at head

office, Dever by name, he has a key, and we were walking towards the Dorchester, and there she was coming out of Barclays Bank counting a small wad.'

'When was this, you say?'

'You don't look too good, old man, sorry I started on this, I suppose, oh about ten days ago.'

'Did you say anything, greet her, anything?'

'I started to bare the choppers but she just looked straight through me. Understood when I'd phoned, in a way, sort of. To hell with the past, including any pal of Ron Beard's, ungreet-worthy swine —'

'What did they tell you on the phone, my phone?'

'There was a hell of a racket, but they said they were living there now and you'd gone off to Rome with an Eyetie bint — sorry, shouldn't have said that. You don't look too good, down that, have a brandy.'

'Leonora's dead,' said Beard. 'She died on the first day of spring.'

'You mean that?' Gregson said. 'Literally, as they say? I mean, not in the sense of she's dead to me and so forth? Though you can't mean it in the other sense, can you now?' He was gaping in his turn.

'It was a mistake,' Beard said. 'You saw somebody like her. After all, it's been a few years since you saw her before. Anybody can make a mistake like that.'

'I could have bloody well sworn —' Gregson called the waiter. 'John, chop chop, *sama sama,* same again. So, dead, is she? Very sorry indeed to hear that, very very sorry I said what I said about her carrying on a bit. There's a Latin thing we learned at school, forgotten it now.'

'*De mortuis nil nisi bonum.*'

'Is that it? Sounds like it. What was the, you know, the trouble then?'

'The thing we all dread but few of us get. It's nothing much to worry about really. Grotesque but comparatively pain-less.'

'Liver? Well, she did knock them back. Well, we all did. Still do, for that matter.' When the drinks arrived he performed an unhandy act of looking at them with distaste. Having sipped then swallowed, he said, more cheerfully: 'They say everybody has a double. That explains it. Not enough faces to go round.' He looked at his watch. 'Where do we go for blot?'

'What?'

'Blotting paper. Lunch. No hurry, of course, but you can't *minum* unless you *makan*. That's one thing I've learned if I've learned nothing else. Did she –?'

'Eat? Oh yes, she ate. She got to like sweet things before the end, cream cakes for breakfast. Very strange. Do you want to eat Italian? You won't eat Italian in this hotel.'

'Well, when in Rome. Spaghetti makes good blot.'

'Spaghetti *make*. Plural.'

'Whatever you say, old man. Whatever you say, old boy, old boy.'

They ate badly but heavily off sauced pasta and thin veal at a *trattoria* round the corner and had a flask of house red, purple really, almost black, before going to drink more gin in the bars of other international hotels. Gregson shivered in the drizzle on their brief walks between bar and bar. When the lights were coming on on the Via Veneto, he said: 'I was thinking of Christmas.'

'Next Christmas or last Christmas?'

'You remember when you wrote those Brunei Christmas carols?' Gregson said. 'Risky thing to put them out on the air but everybody who knew English was too pissed to be listening. What was that one with the Sultan in it? You know, to the tune of Wenceslas?'

Beard sang to the wet bright street:

> 'Sultan Omar Ali Saifuddin
> From a ten-cent stamp looked
> At white men eating Christmas pudden,
> Though they hot and damp looked.

> Sweat lay on them while they lay
> > In the arms of Bacchus,
> Which made S.O.A.S. say:
> > I think Christmas cra-ack-ers.'

'Those were the days,' Gregson said. 'Pink gins, *molto* biggo,' he then said, since they were now in a bar, to the barman. 'Christmas. You remember old Leonora getting stripped stark ballock and diving into old Banks's swimming-pool and coming out covered with leeches?'

'Was it stark ballock? I don't remember.'

'All on show, old man. Sorry, shouldn't bring back the past. Why not, though? All we have, the past. Men of our age. Not much of a future really.'

'Speak for yourself, Greg. I'm making a new start. I've got a big film thing on at the moment.'

'Who's in it, Gina whatshername?' He looked with drunken envy on Beard, widower, Eyetie bint, film stars, *la dolce vita*. And then: 'How about us trying a couple of the local bints, the ones with big tits and little dogs?'

'Not for me. I'm faithful.'

'That's a laugh. A free man and faithful.'

'When you're in love you're not really free.'

A fat middleaged American, whose buttocks overflowed his barstool, turned to Beard on this and said: 'You can say that again.'

'When you're in love,' Beard began to repeat, but Gregson said:

'It's only to a wife you're unfaithful. Infidelity's a technical term, sort of.'

'You can say that again.'

'Marriage,' Beard said, 'is complex semiotics, but love is indefinable.' It was time to be going: this epigrammatic phase could not be easily sustained. He saw himself in the mirror behind the bar – getting old and talking about love. '*Satu empat jalan*,' he said.

'That means,' said Gregson to the American, 'one for road.

Satu is one and *empat* is four and *jalan* is road. Malay, that is. Sort of a white man's joke. Look,' he said fiercely to Beard, 'you're not going now. I stopped over to get pissed with you for old time's sake, didn't I?'

'Got to get back.'

'But there's nobody there, you said. You said she'd gone off.'

'Got to get back. May be a phone call. Poor little girl, getting shot at by the bloody Arabs.'

'You can say that again.'

When Gregson had more or less passed out, Beard remained sufficiently capable to tell the taxi-driver where he lived. The taxi-driver did not know the piazza, but he knew Da Meo Patacca, so that was all right. Arriving in front of the apartment building, Beard looked up at the Roman moon, newly emerged after many nights' occlusion, and saw the light on on the top floor – her, their, apartment. He had left it on then, how? Couldn't have, went out in daylight. Christ Jesus, she was back, the war had been called off, he should have read the newspapers instead of wasting a day with that stupid bastard Greg. Or the war was still on but women photographers forbidden to attend. Such thoughts panted through his mind as he fought his way past a small van parked at the street door or *portone*, on which things, personal effects, things were being loaded by a couple of haired jeaned young Romans. Mounting the stairs too fast, Beard bumped into another youth bearing down what looked like a soap box overflowing with books. '*Scusi.*' Somebody moving, doing literal moonlight flit. Beard could see, on the turn leading to the last pitch, his their own door open and light flowing out. Near death, he drank litres of air while his heart two-fisted at him. Then he did the last flight on legs that were both painful and non-existent, calmed his heart as best he could outside the door, then, trying to find air for the greeting *tesoro* or *darling* and failing, tottered in. The passage looked curiously nude. He went into the diningroom and saw a man's back. The man was telephoning. In English. 'Will do,' he said. 'No sweat. Bye now.' He turned, showing himself to be P. R. Pathan. 'Who the hell are you?' Pathan said, nasty and corrugated, quite unlike his Jerry Bauer dust-jacket portrait. 'Out, whoever you bloody well are.'

There was absolutely no furniture at all in the room except a telephone and two chairs. Beard sat on the one of the latter that was nearer the door. No hurry, take your time, lots of breath needed. Gathering it, Beard made hand movements that could, he supposed, be interpreted as apologetic. 'Give me a –' he tried. Pathan took the telephone off the other chair, sat on the chair, took out a pack of Marlboro, lighted one, sneered out some smoke. Then he said:

'Ah. Is that yours in the back room there, that crap about Byron? Are you living with her? You, is it, you? Christ.' It was a patrician accent with a certain weakness of the *r*. Cghvap about Byghvon. So that farting acronym was perhaps self-mockery. Chghvist. 'Scraping the barrel, I'd say. But you're not doing so well, friend. As you'll see, as you'll see. Or not, of course. She may be blown to buggery in the Holy Land.'

'How did you –'

'Know? Photograph of brave press folk boarding at Fiumicino in this morning's *Mondiale*. Little Powliwowly grinning away there, off to a kosher blood-gorge. Or halal blood-gorge.'

'No such.'

'No such thing, right. Bit of a stickler for exactitude, eh? Subliterary men are usually like that. Anyway, she's gone, but it wouldn't have made any bloody difference whether she was here or not. Lock her in the bloody *gabinetto*. What's mine's mine and everything here's mine. Not a sodding thing in this flat that hasn't been paid for with my money, mate.'

'How did you –'

'Get in? Lived here once, lawful husband, right? Could live here still if I wanted, which is the last flaming thing in the world I'd think of, I can tell you. Still have the key, then. Don't need it any more, though. There.' He threw it at Beard. 'Now you've got two keys. Any more questions?'

'I haven't.'

'Asked any yet, correct. While you're panting you can pant a bit more. She's a bitch, a bitch, a bloody bitch. Pant at that. As well as with shock and horror and outrage at me walking in, just like that, and being bloody vindictive, which is what I am being. But don't utter any word, when you can, about illegal breaking and entering. I got the divorce, not she. A Trinidad divorce. Desertion. But it doesn't run here, no. As far as the Italians are concerned I'm still the boss and all's mine. So don't go ringing up the Questura. When you have breath to do it, that is. Or Italian, for that matter. Do you have any Italian? Except for *amore* and *tesoro* and the rest of the crap?'

'You assume,' Beard said, 'that I –'

'Someone chucked two of my books in the garbage can. I assume it was you. You know who I am all right. And you're somebody who writes things for the great crappy demotic media.'

'If you've touched that script of mine. Or that typewriter. I'll bloody well –'

'No you'll bloody well not. Colonial wog that I am I'll have your white balls dangling from the ends of my strong brown fingers.'

'You're a bastard,' Beard said. 'That much is certain, you bastard. She was right about that, you bastard.'

'Crisp nervous dialogue. Don't use many words, but repeat the ones you do use. Lesson number one, as administered to Scott Fitzgerald and William Faulkner.' Pathan smashed his smoked-out cigarette with his presumed Gucci heel but, strangely, put the end in an ashtray. He then set about lighting a new one. 'Or to Saul Bellow for that matter.'

'I didn't know Saul Bellow worked in films. Still, a kind of precognition, everything explained in time, cleanliness of fundament and so on. What were we talking about? Ah yes, you're a bastard, Prrrrp, or whatever you farting well like to be called, but I've genuinely admired some of the things you've written. That's why it's all such a pity.'

'Look, you, Scriptman, or whatever your bleeding nonentity's name is, you're drunk, aren't you? Not taking much of this lot in, are you? She's a bitch, I tell you, and a bloody bitch, and I don't know whether it's better for it to happen to an old man like you or a young one like me.'

'Youngish. I looked you up in the public library. Hammersmith. As for me being old, I bet I have more teeth than you have, you brownish bastard.'

'Ah, colour coming out now, eh? I might have expected it.'

'*You* started the colour business, saying you'd pull my white balls off. I caught what you said, brownish bastard, about her being a bitch and so on. Well, that's a highly subjective term, as your hero Saul Bellow might say, and if she was a bitch to you it's because you were a bastard to her, so try that one out. All I know is that I love her.'

'Jesus, old man's love. I never said I admired Saul Bellow. He's a Jew, and what can I learn from a Jew? Love, eh? That probably means you were lonely and despised and not getting it regular and she comes along and says you can put it in if you like. That's how it happened, isn't it, and now you think you're in lerv, stupid idiot. Well, I give you fair warning.' As in orchestration of the phrase, a motor horn sounded petulantly from below. Pathan went to the window and yelled down: '*Aspettate. Un attimo. Vengo subito.*' He did not trouble to switch off his British genteel accent. He turned back to Beard and said: 'Ungrateful Roman bastards. Furnishing a flat for the young bastards and that's the thanks you get.'

'How do you classify the Romans? White, are they? White-balled? Another thing, Fart or whatever you like to be called, you're not supposed to be here. You're supposed to be in New York pretending to be a professor.'

'Knew that, did you? None of your bloody business, I'd say. Couldn't stand the job, if you insist on knowing. Black poems about tearing the white man's balls off.'

'Ah, interesting. Privilege of the brown man, is that it?'

'Blacks, I can't stand blacks, I can't stand their fucking black ignorant arrogance. I spoke out if you must know.'

'Ah,' Beard said. 'Was that before or after that great big arrogant black bitch of a Wimpy or Limpy or whatever she's called walked out on you?' He was not, so he seemed to be telling himself, a script-writer for nothing. 'Saw her yesterday in Trastevere here with a rich-looking white-balled waddler, bastard that you are. Can't get it up was what I heard. Drunk and impotent was the way it was put to me. Go down there now and start lugging all that stuff up again. You've no bloody right to – I'm going to have a look to see precisely what – Good God, bastard that you are, even the pictures off the walls. Even the television and the bookshelves.' He got up to go into the bedroom, but Pathan leapt on him. Beard turned in surprise to find himself clutched in brownish hands, the end of a Marlboro wagging at him. Pathan cried from either side of the cigarette:

'Why I don't call those boys up here this instant to tear you and piss on that bloody stupid script of yours in there I don't know.' He slapped Beard on the cheek but gently, as if to revive him. 'It's because I'm sorry for you, that's what it is I suppose. Christ bloody well help me, you too for that matter. Thank Christ I have the consolation of my art, which is more than you have, bloody stupid script-writer.' Beard found that, though clutched, he could quite easily move into the bedroom. There he found the bedstead gone as also the mirror and dressing-table, though the mattress, with bedclothes roughly retossed on it, was still there. He said to Pathan, who was spitting out his cigarette-end though still manually attached to Beard:

'You've taken every bloody thing. Have you taken even her bloody clothes?'

'One of those Roman boys wanted them for some bloody reason of his own. I told him she was small, the little bitch, but he said the smaller the better.'

Beard removed Pathan's claws without trouble. 'I made that bed this morning,' he said. 'Hurt, don't you, you like to hurt, you bastard. Do you realize there's nothing of her here left at all so far as I can damn well see, blast you?' The horn sounded very loud from below again. Pathan picked up his fag-end and ran to the front room and then to its window. He called, in his genteel British accent, very foul Italian:

'*Madonna impestata, vaffnculo, stronzi, merda, aspettate. Vengo* bloody *subito,* blasted *farabutti.*' He turned back to Beard, saying: 'Impatient ungrateful little Roman swine. I give them a flat and I furnish it for them and that's the bloody thanks –'

'*You* furnish it? How about that poor little girl getting shot at, swine your bloody self. Ah,' seeing, not script-writer for nothing. 'Pederastic set-up, is it, is that what it's all about?'

'It is what it is and none of your business,' Pathan said. 'But let me tell you this, whatever your name is, secretive aren't you, not that I give a monkey's left ballock –'

'What colour is a monkey's left –'

'I'm off tomorrow. London, got a book to promote, more than you can say for yourself, but I'll be back, ah yes. And I'll gloat in one sense and in another not. You heard about Judith and Holofernes?'

'Now, how did that –' Beard began, astonished.

'Of course, great bible-readers, you script hacks, all fucking and fighting and words of one syllable. Judith and Holofernes, Salome and John the Baptist, same story.'

'There I beg to –'

'A man's prick, a man's head. They used to call a prick a holofernes, did you know that, no of course you didn't, that's asking too much. But that's all they want, a man's head. Black or grey, makes fuck-all difference. You'll come home one night to find her with another one she took pity on. Probably shagging with a syphilitic Arab now, I shouldn't wonder. Me, lonely brown writer in wet bloody London, and I talked about love too, stupid bastard that you are, should know better at your age. Well, you'll find out. Or if you're wise you'll listen to me now. She's gone, right? And there's nothing of her here left. Not even a smell of her, except on those bloody bed-sheets.

She doesn't exist. Get out now. Stay the night at the Grand, and tomorrow morning –'

'Funny thing, just been staying the day there, friend of mine from –'

'That's where I'll be when I've sorted out those Roman hooligans below. Sort of cleanse myself of this bloody place. I can see it all over again, all happening all over again. Ugh.'

'In bed with somebody, was she?' Script-writer. 'In bed, say, with a –' Pathan looked bitterly and said:

'Easy for you, isn't it? All you have to do is to write down Scene Ninety-two or whatever the hell it is, medium close shot or some such bloody mumbo-jumbo, a bed, slow tracking shot to close-up of heads on pillow, one is hers, the other that of a –'

'You must get over this colour business,' Beard said.

'And you get bloody well paid for it too, I know, leaving all the work to the actors and cameramen and director, and the rest of the crap-bags. But I have to get it all down, all out, all the agony of it.' The hornblowers below, unabashed, were at it again. 'Rest, rest, perturbed spirit,' Pathan said sadly.

'You mean me?'

'I mean nothing and nobody. But take my advice and get out.' Pathan had had the curious decency not to put cigarette ends on the floor but into an ashtray bearing the name of the Hotel Carlton, Cannes. He now emptied the ashtray out of the window. He then pocketed the ashtray. 'That's the lot, then,' he said. Then he left, clomping rather. Beard went out to watch him go down, thinking of shouting *bastard* and *swine* into the stairwell but then thinking better of it, the lateness of the hour, consideration for neighbours. He went back in, slamming the door. The van down below was trying to start without success, the effect being that of a man trying to stir seedless loins to action, or rake for phlegm that wasn't there. Pathan was using words like *stupido* and *cretino* with his patrician British accent. Then the van started and they were away. Mad, Pathan was evidently mad. And he, Beard, how was he? Angry, yes, but also amazed and not a little frightened. Had not Paola said something about indenting the natural order, and might not this be the beginning of it? Also, of course, lonely as hell again. He stripped himself naked and went to lie with the messed-up sheets on the mattress on the floor. His penis had swollen and arisen like some avenging rod. He grasped it fiercely and frotted away, trying to evoke Paola's image, though with difficulty. It was like trying to evoke the image of someone who did not exist. There were other images available, of course — film-stars chiefly, most of them either very old or very dead. A loud female voice at Da Meo Patacca was singing, plangently, that song about the funicular railway. Beard saw Gregson in the Yacht Club in Brunei Town doing his drunken parody of that song, heard him:

> 'Smash it, crash it, bash it on the floor,
> Wham it, slam it, jam it in the door.'

A fair exorcism. Beard felt the room going gently round so, his limp hand dropping from the limp thing, forced himself to sleep.

The telephone woke him. He wondered at first why he could not get out of bed, then ceased to wonder, as also at the lack of obstacles on his dark path, towards the ringing. Paola in Israel, just back from photographing night-fighting, calling from the King David in Jerusalem, say. '*Pronto*,' Beard said breathily.

'Greg here. Greg Greg. Why did you bugger off like that? Come back here at once.'

'Do you know what time it is?' Beard squinted at his wrist-watch, reading three in the morning from the light outside. 'Besides, you passed out, remember?'

'Well, I'm up and about again, having a noggin with a wog. Talk about a coincidence, old boy, old boy. Come back here and have the shit talked out of you good and proper, as they say.'

'You mean Pathan? Told you all, has he? About the ageing script-writer in love?'

'I had a clerk called Pathan, you remember? Tamil, black as the ace of. Told this one that. Then he goes on about white bastards. Then about black bastards. Agreed with him there. All right really. A writer. And it was his Eyetie bint before you got her. Talk about a coincidence. Come on over, then.'

'Why don't you go to bloody bed? You've got an early plane tomorrow, today.'

'Might as well stay up, get poured on to it. Sleep all the way to Singapore. You coming or not coming?'

'Not coming.'

'You never were much of a bloody pal. Never had it off with her, you know that? In vino veritability or whatever the hell it is. Any consolation to you is it to know that? Not for lack of trying, old boy old boy. Didn't fancy me, that's all. Well, all over now. So you say. But I saw her near the bloody Dorchester, can you believe that?'

'I'm hanging up.'

'Do that, you sod. You're in a bad way, though, remember what I said. Not half the man you were, you bugger. Now *I'm* hanging u —'

Beard cut him off before the initiation of the plosive. Then he noticed his erection swinging in the street-glow. Vast, chordee-like, the fruit of alcohol. He took it back with him to the mattress on the floor and was not surprised to find the image of Miriam ready to be invoked. She was about the age she must be about now, about forty, no age at all, and though maturer and fuller-fleshed she gave the wall-fruit kisses of her young, though three-striped, innocence. She had not advanced even to the rank of staff-sergeant. The uniform came off at once and in one piece, rather like the evening-dress shrouds used in the 'leave-taking' salons of Forest Lawn, and there was no War Department lingerie beneath. Beard devoured her like a hungry dog and shot his bolt growling. Then he lay back *triste*, in shame. What a mess he had made of his life. What a curse sex was. How absurd and degrading this attempt to turn Byron and the Shelleys into dream-stuff for gawping hand-holding gum-chewers in the dark. He had achieved nothing except an award, a Japanese epicene figurine called Terry, for the best foreign, to Japan that was, dramatic script of the year. He considered himself in love with a girl for whom it was more proper for him to conceive a parental attitude. Not that that would let him off any hook, for incest, as a grey-haired Warner Brothers man had told him gravely, having done computer work on film trends, was the coming dominant theme. Always had been in a sense, though disguised. Think of *Daddy Long-legs, The Seventh Veil* and so on. What a bloody mess. Such corruption. Was it perhaps proper for him to wish to die? Death in Rome, with those stairs outside a ready and waiting instrument thereof.

Corruption? The poet Belli apologized to the Sultan of Brunei for being unable to take his top hat off in the royal presence. The unity of the sculptor's conception and execution, he explained. He sang in a tobacco-stained Roman tenor, to the tune of 'Here we come a-wassailing', certain words written long before by Ronald Beard and broadcast when the English-speaking population of Brunei had been too pissed to be listen-ing:

'Here we come a-pocketing
   Our lawful Christmas bribes.
Prices are a-rocketing
   So all the Chinese tribes
Must put more in our banks,
Be more generous with their thanks,
And we'll give them the contracts they so heartily desire,
And we'll all be well off when we retire.'

Four

Beard was able more clearly to see, the following morning, which was another wettish one, the extent of the alleged repossession carried out by Pathan and his Romans. Everything mobile had left the kitchen, with the exception of the gas cooker. There were no tables or cupboards in any of the rooms. Paola had nothing either to wear or to re-read, since even her well-saved newspapers and magazines had been, it would seem, used for wrapping fragile lamp-stands in. Beard's script, typewriter, paper, eraser and reference books had been spared, but he would have to compose dialogue on his knee, ridiculous. There were two loose bookshelves, however, which had been rejected or overlooked, and it was possible to place these across the kitchen sink and type with the taps looking on, dripping ironic encouragement. He saw that keenly enough before he did anything about it. There were other things to do first: find out from the *Mondiale* how things were in Israel with Paola, but there was a hell of a language problem; obey a cable that had arrived before eight and, indeed, woken Beard up. The cable was from Ed Schaumwein, to whom he had given an address but not a telephone number, and it said that Hill was definitely going to direct and required as much draft script as possible as soon as possible. This meant that Beard would have to get Xeroxed what he had already done, since he kept no carbons, and cope with whatever bureaucratic idiocies were entailed in the sending of a parcel of typescript from Rome to Los Angeles. The third thing was to get those photographic prints, one way of proving that Paola had certainly existed the day before yesterday.

But first the telephone. It was, in a way, a relief when it rang as he approached it, whatever fatuities or horrors it had waiting for him, since he was thus able to postpone the agony of formulating Italian questions. Answers were a different matter: you could always say *non capisco*. He lifted the receiver and said '*Pronto.*'

'Missed the bloody plane, man. Meant to have an hour on the bed and the silly Eyetie sods forgot to wake me. Greg Greg here, by the way. Just having hair of the dog. Come over and get pissed.'

'No. No. No. Is that swine Pathan still there?'

'Who? Pathan's in Brunei Town, black scheming bastard. What made you think of – Oh, that other one. No, he's gone off just now as a matter of, saw him paying his bill as I went to the bar, looked right through me, snooty bugger. Should never have given them their independence. Whip them. Tread on them. Sort of language they understand. So come on round here and get –'

'No, I tell you, blast you. That swine took everything. A glass of cold water in a plastic toothmug – my breakfast, that was.'

'Come round and have breakfast here, though it's a bit late now for breakfast, but come round anyway. Thought I'd stay on a bit. Rather taken a fancy to the place.'

'What?'

'Can't get a booking for a couple of days and even then it would be on some sort of bloody immigration plane to Sydney, Eyetie workers seeking the promised land. First class, I told them, to Singapore and no bloody nonsense. Have to wait, they say. Don't mind waiting. Rather taken a fancy to the –'

'How's the war going?'

'War? War's bloody over, man. Oh, the yid-wog war you mean. Not seen the paper yet. Knocking hell out of each other, fratricidal bastards, shouldn't wonder. You know they're the same race really, yids and wogs? No foreskins, no pork. That's why I say fratricidal. Too early though for intellectual conversation, old boy old boy. Come round here and get –'

'No. I've things to do.'

'Knew you'd say that. So I've got a Hertz car all lined up and I'm coming round there, what do you think about that, sod that you are?'

'I won't be in. Besides, you don't know where I am.'

'Are you bloody bonkers? Course I know where you are. Got it written down here. Only a matter of keeping leaning out of this bloody Fiat that's coming round and saying loud and clear Piassa Santa Whatsit, and then they point. Easy.'

'So that bastard Pathan gave you the address, did he?'

'Had it already, old boy old boy, but sort of lost it. Now it's here before me writ large as they say. So get ready. Greg Greg is a-coming, ha ha. *Selamat*.' He hung up.

Beard looked sourly at the telephone. He didn't quite know how to put his question about Paola to the *Mondiale* and he didn't know who to ask for there, and he foreknew that he would be unable to understand the load of Italian thrown at him. Later, think about it. Do it later. He put his pages of script into the soft leather zippered case he used for putting scripts in, then found his raincoat, which was all mixed up with the bed-sheets. Ready to leave, he heard the telephone ring again. Bloody Greg.

'I'm going out now, you idiot,' Beard said. 'I don't know when I'll be back.'

'Mr Beard? Mr Ronald Beard?'

'Of course it damn well is, you stupid.' And then: 'Oh, I beg your – I thought it was –' For it was a woman's voice, British, impersonal, wafted faintly through a loud noise of grilling.

'This is London. Mrs Beard is on the line.'

'What? There must be some – *Mrs*?' And then he heard the authentic voice of Leonora, faint but clear, cultured though Welshy. She half-sang half-recited one of Beard's Brunei carols. He listened, his mouth open almost to its limit.

> 'Brunei night, unholy night –
> Dogs howl, mosquitoes bite.

Brown men busy with axes and knives,
White men sleeping with other men's wives.
The curry's making me cough.
There's nothing to do but eff off.'

Then silence save for the kitchen noises. He held the instrument in a hand whose tremor he was able objectively to admire. The dialling tone started. He clattered it on to its stand. Greg, bloody Greg. But how? No, wait. Trenchmore. Not Trenchmore but one of the Trenchmore children. In the Hammersmith house there was still most of Beard's gear, including Uher tape-recorder and tapes. Many tapes, Radio Brunei tapes, personal tapes, silly drunken tapes. What was the name of that eldest Trenchmore child, the daughter? Nasty little bitch, cold green eyes of malice. Deirdre? Dymphna? Augusta? Something Irish anyway. He must give Trenchmore hell, letting her do that. Dial London. He groaned at the known arithmetical agony of the task. Later. Or ignore it? Later.

But God, the shock of it. He needed brandy and there was no brandy. Out out. He tottered out. Voice from the dead. But nothing horrifying about that any more. He had put on a series called *Voices of the Dead* in Brunei, with the help of Radio Malaya's archives, starting with Robert Browning trying to recite 'How they brought the good news from Aix to Ghent' and messing it up. Most frartflah sorrah forgotten me own varses. There were some dead more alive now than they had been when they were alive. Humphrey Bogart, for instance. Nothing evil about a voice from the dead. Just the shock, that's all. And anger and puzzlement. Outside on the wet cobbles he ceased to totter. He stalked to the little bar round the corner and had two large espressos and two large brandies. Not cognac, Brandy Stock, its *gusto* advertised as *morbido*, meaning only soft, but you could not easily kill the English connotation. Its morbid gust burnt his heart. He ate a sweet pastry and remembered how Leonora had taken to sweet pastries, though with a light gin accompaniment, in mid-morning. He had another large espresso. Morbid leather case under right arm, he stalked to the photographic place behind Da Meo Patacca and had to wait. Then he was given a big buff *busta*. As for *pagamento*, she would pay when she returned. She was going to return, then. She existed. Her little quick hands and clever eye were inside what he now tucked into his case to nest with the partial script he must now take to be copied. How, he asked the young photographic men, was the war in Israel going? They went *boooooh* in the Roman manner, meaning they neither knew nor cared. Beard left. Then the *scippatori* struck.

It was part of Roman culture – two young grinners on a Vespa or Lambretta, coming in suddenly from the rear, the pillion-boy making the grab, then off, triumphant, waving, grinning, holding trophy aloft. 'Christ,' Beard yelled in English, gesturing, head-shaking, going mad, 'There's nothing in there worth anything to you, stupid young bastards.' They would get a hundred lire for the morbid case, they would throw script and photographs into the bloody Tiber. 'Stupid young.' He ran after them towards the piazza, their machine, which had no *targa* of identification, farting and belching Romanly at him, they not now just grinning but guffawing. Fine Roman predatory teeth, vapid bloody insolent Roman bloody handsomeness and useless idiotic youth. He yelled. '*Furbi. Farabutti.*' They moved, against horns and operatic cries, towards the Via Santa Cecilia, not giving a damn about its being a *senso unico* and them going the wrong way. 'Stop the bastards, crash into the bastards,' Beard tried to yell, though lacking breath. To his surprise a Fiat-driver obeyed. The Fiat drove, firmly if slowly, right at them. The *scippatori* were very surprised. They were excreting bad words, the pillion-boy waving Beard's case like a proposed floppy weapon, the handlebar one trying to back, turn, back, swerve, veer, The Fiat jerked its nose at them and they went down. Beard was there now, wheezing as if he would die. Greg Greg got out of the Fiat, saying: 'Whip them, tread on them, put the little swine back under colonial rule.' He kicked at them vigorously, though, or because, they were down. Beard got his muddied case and clutched it in both hands.

There were now many around, loud and gesturing, as well as an endless file of honking cars. There were no police, they being busy elsewhere. Greg yelled at the honkers: 'Shut up, where are your bloody manners?' He went on kicking. Beard grabbed a handful of thick black fat coarse Roman male hair then let it go. The young scoundrels were at work on a fantasy duet in which God and God's mother and son were bizarrely involved in plague, syphilis, lavatories and human genitalia. Greg let them get to their feet, then began slapping them. 'Feed them to the lions in the Hippodrome or Colosseum or whatever it is. Make them do an honest day's work, sell the bastards into slavery. Know their type. Wogs, wops. No good even for coolie labour. And shut that dirty language up, I know it's dirty. *Diam*,' he yelled to the swelling chorus of honkers. 'Bloody well *diam*, the lot of you.'

'Let them go,' Beard said. 'Enough.'

'Enough? Young swine. Ah.' Greg had noticed something. A large russet-stained chunk of ancient Roman stone, detached from some long-vanished monument of imperial oppression, lay outside the greengrocer's shop. He picked it up in both hands and started to damage the *scippatori*'s Vespa with it. 'Not well made these things,' he panted. 'Like putty. Used to have the agency for them, remember. Back in Brunei.' The two scoundrelly youths would have opened Greg's throat with their teeth had not a fat woman, perhaps their mother or aunt or cousin's mother, now appeared to belabour them, pulsing out a magnificent tragic aria at the same time. Seeing what Greg was doing, though, she started to belabour him, too, but Greg would stand no nonsense. 'Ah no,' he said. 'Not having that, missis.' He threatened her with a chunk of her own city. He addressed the crowd, which was sizeable, having first yelled a *diam* at the honkers. 'Grow up,' he told them. 'Learn to stand on your own feet. Try and be a bit more bloody intelligent. You won't always have the white man to lean on. All right. All over.' He got back into the Fiat. Beard said:

'There, just there,' pointing. 'No need to give me a lift. Just

there, see. Park there.' And Beard went into the corner tobacconist's to buy Mercator panatelas and a small box of thumb-
tacks. There were loud words for him, but whether of sympathy,
felicitation or reproach was not easy to tell. It was not
right for native *scippatori* to rob foreigners, but neither was it
right for foreigners to trounce native *scippatori*. A proud
people, very keen on regional loyalty. The Trasteverines even
had an annual self-glorification, crammed with *caroselli*, Tunis-
ian carpetmongers, murderously amplified singers, which they
called the *Festa de Noi Antri*, meaning the feast of us others,
us, ourselves, none else, blast you. There were loud words for
him in the bar next door but one, where he bought a bottle of
Brandy Stock and begged the loan of two glasses. Robbed, he
told them, of everything. You got it back again, they seemed to
cry, and you trounced them into the bargain. No, stupids, this
was another robbery. He went back to the apartment building to see dimly Gregson lugging a big box upstairs.

'How far are you. Jesus. Up? Bloody stairs. Not used to.'

'You're approaching the top of the first flight. Five more
flights to go. Take it very easy. Bad for the heart.'

'You're. Telling me it's. Jesus. Booze. Goes down easy. Goes
up hard. It's. Give us a bloody.'

Beard gave him a hand. On top of bottles was a pile of newspapers and magazines, all in English. CRISIS IN SINAI
DESERT, said *The Times*. They went up chassé-wise, a mime of
a slowly mobile coat of arms. Outside the apartment door,
Beard searching for his key, they each near died on his feet.
They kicked the box inside, dying, then lay a space on the floor,
head to head. The telephone rang. 'You,' groaned Beard. 'You
nearer.' Greg crawled to the instrument, which was on the
floor anyway, and Beard crawled after. 'Aaargh,' Greg said into
the mouthpiece. Then: 'Oo? Who? Aaargh.' He beckoned that
Beard should take over. 'Told you she was. Knew she was.
Take.'

'Mrs?'

'Yeah. Told you.'

Beard, too exhausted to tremble anew, listened. Leonora sang:

> 'Come all ye crawlers,
> Psychosycophantic,
> Purr and defer to the State Treasurer.
> Give him a parcel
> And then kiss his arcel.
> Pay homage at the Yacht Club,
> That snottier-than-snot club,
> Give pleasure to your treasure,
> The Treaaas-ur-er.'

Then, as before, a frying silence. Beard carefully put the receiver down. When able to speak, he said:

'You know all about this, don't you? The Brunei Christmas carols. You started all that off, didn't you?'

'Don't get that. Don't know what you mean. But it was her, wasn't it? Great big nasty joke of yours that, in very bad taste. About she being, you know. Where is she anyway?'

'Scattered. She's ashes. She's dead. That was her voice, true. Recorded though. She sang that thing. State Treasurer of Brunei.'

'That swine. Ah, that carol. She sang that? Funny. Very funny coincidence. Queer sort of thing to do, that. Rings up to sing that. Perhaps it's to annoy. Having a go at you. Nothing to do with me, old man. No need to look at me like that, is there?'

'There's something bloody funny going on,' Beard said. 'How do I know you're not tied up in it?'

'I'll say there's something bloody funny going on,' said Greg. They were both still half reclined on the floor. 'You're here in this dump and not an ounce of furniture to be seen.'

'She exists, I tell you.'

'I keep telling you she exists. I saw her with my own eyes, didn't I? Let's have a drink. These are for you, these papers, but perhaps I'm not too happy about buying them, seeing you're so bloody ungrateful and accusing. Said you wanted the news. Well, there it is.'

'Paola exists, I mean. What you call my Eyetie bint. But Leonora's dead. I saw her die, damn you.'

'No fridge, I suppose. But I suppose they didn't cart off the water supply. I'm going to have a whisky *ayer*. I brought glasses.'

'So did I.'

'That's all right, then.'

Beard gave himself a long swig of Brandy Stock, then a long swig of tap-water. He took the prints of Paola's photographs out of their buff *busta*. Some were coloured, some black and white. Why? Dear girl. Dear sweet talented girl. He began thumb-tacking them up in the terribly bare living-room.

'See what you mean, old man. Drive you up the bloody wall, these walls I mean. Naked, I mean. Like a bloody prison. Could I ring somebody up to send round some ice?'

'If you want. I don't know anybody that would.'

'What's the Italian for ice anyway?'

'*Ghiaccio.*'

'Ghee atch oh. Right.' Greg went over to the open window and looked down. 'Ah, a bloke in a white coat down there takings cups of coffee on a tray. Eh, boy, you, Jewseppy, bring up *ayer batu*, ghee atch oh that is, damn silly language, chop chop toot sweet. Ghee atch oh *sini lekas-lekas*, comprenny, *chepat sa-kali* and put some *jildi* in it.' He waved a ten-thousand lire note. 'He'll bring it,' he said, turning round to thumb-tacking Beard. 'A matter of going the right way about it. Get anything you want if you do.'

'You're right about me being bloody ungrateful,' Beard said. 'If it hadn't been for you they'd have gone forever. My script there and these.'

'There'd be the negatives. '

'The negatives are here in this *busta*. So I'm grateful, you see. There.' The room was filling nicely with oblique views of Rome. But Gregson was looking out of the window again, saying:

66

'Those fat-arsed cherub things across there. What's it all in aid of?'

'That's where she's supposed to be buried. In the crypt in there. Saint Cecilia, matron saint of music.'

'I don't see what those fat-arsed cherubs have got to do with it. Typical Roman, I suppose. Fat arses everywhere. Bellies too. All that spaghetti.'

'*Those* spaghetti.'

'Don't think I care much for the place after all. Seen as much as I want to see.'

'Christ man, all you've seen is an international hotel bar and this bare slummy flat.'

'And those bare-arsed cherub arrangements. What's it all about anyway? A big sort of RC HQ.'

'That's the Vatican. Rome is very pagan really. It's also supposed to be very beautiful.'

'Heathen beauty, eh? I've got a sort of heathen beauty waiting for me back there. *Ship me somewheres east of Suez where the best is like the worst.* That ice is a bloody long time coming. How about a bit of blot? No *minum* without *makan*.'

'There.' Beard had finished his tacking. 'She's here now. She's with me. She exists. I suppose it'll be safe for us to go and eat in the Rugantino.'

'What do you mean, safe?'

'I don't suppose anybody would break in and steal this lot.'

'Are you cracked, man? Are you properly bloody cracked?'

As they went out into the piazza, which weak sunlight now drenched, Gregson saw the boy from whom he had ordered ice, white-aproned, bearing thimbles of espresso on a tray, hardly worth the journey. 'You know what you can do with your ghee aitch whatever it is. Up your coalhole, greasy wog, wop, I mean.' The lad jeered and made an old Roman sign.

'You mean *culo*.'

'He knows what I mean, idle young bastard.'

It was the Rugantino's day of weekly repose, so its locked

doors told them, so they had to eat at the Comparone. 'Those scampi are a bit off,' Gregson said, having eaten them. 'This wine's like pure malt vinegar.'

'Hardly malt. Hardly pure.'

'Right. What are those little black things it's full of?'

'Wine-flies they're called, I think.'

'This piece of veal or whatever they call it is exactly the shape of the sole of a size nine boot, see. What are those squashy things there?'

'*Zucchini.*'

Gregson looked like a man making a decision. He chewed some of the day before yesterday's bread and then announced: 'I'm off. I'm on my way. I've done all for you that I can do.'

'I'm certainly grateful that you turned up at the right time when those young louts tried to *scippo* my –'

'Don't mean just that. Anyway, I've had enough. Next flight east, whatever it is. Rome, you can keep it.'

'You're not coming back to finish the booze off? There's a hell of a lot of bottles.'

'Beer and tonic water mostly, old man. And just catch me climbing those sodding stairs again. Jesus, what sort of a life is it for you? You don't even have a lift there. The only stairs you'll find me climbing from now on are those with an air hostess's legs at the top. You're in a bad way, I tell you. What in God's name are you going to do?'

'Wait. Write my script and wait.'

Greg looked at the bill as if it were another uneatable course. 'I've done my best,' he said. 'You can't deny that, old man.'

'I don't get you.'

'Never mind. Look, if you want that thing there copied and sent off, they'll do it for you at the Grand. Special business-man's facility. Put it on my bill if you like. They'll do it while I'm packing. There must be something moving east of Suez before the day's out.'

So they walked back jaggedly to the parked hired Fiat, which had not been visited with revenge from the trounced *scippatori*. There were too many Fiats of the same size, and it would have been a fatiguing task to scratch VAFFNCULO on all of them, the tyres having first been ravaged. Gregson drove eccentrically to the Via Veneto, shouting rebukes at pedestrians and fellow-drivers alike, and found at the Grand Hotel that there was a flight to the Lebanon at six. 'That'll do,' he said. 'Beirut. There'll be a lot of things flying east from Beirut. Nice little airport bar at Beirut.'

Beard had his script copied and the copy dispatched to dear Ed at Warner Brothers, Burbank, California. Something achieved, anyway. He gladly agreed to see Greg off at Fiumicino. The least he could do. A couple of drinks in the bar and then watch him go off. After that wait. There was just a chance. There was always a chance. At a cross-roads, if you waited, you never knew. A mad secret chance. But he foresaw himself going back to Trastevere, alone to aloneness. 'Gin and tonic for two and a kichey drop of *merah*, Malay for red that is, meaning angostura. Yes, large ones, *molto* grando, and not that local muck there, Pissfords or whatever it's called. Gordon's. *A Gordon forrr me, a Gordon forrr me, if ye're nae a Gordon ye're nae guid to me*,' Gregson sang. Other drinkers in the dark bar looked at Gregson and shrugged. A woman looked at Gregson and then at Beard, and then again at Beard. Beard looked at her and his eyes beat like supernumerary hearts. It could not be that Paola had crept back to Rome merely to drink in its airport bar, hiding in the dark the fact that she had grown older, fatter, no not fatter, fuller, more matronly, hoping also that Beard had forgotten her, wide-eyed at the fulfilment of the hope, since here he was too at the airport bar, ready for a journey. There were three full bar-stools between her and Greg, four between her and him. She wore some sort of uniform tunic, though with no badge or stripe of rank, she wore pressed slacks, she had what looked like a negroni in front of her. Beard now saw what Greg Greg's function was. Why, then, was he performing the function so ham-handedly?

He should not have saved Paola's pictures, thus asserting her existence. Beard felt a hopeless chill suffuse him. Had he done that because that was all there would ever now be of Paola, and there was no danger of her ever getting in the way of the resurrection of the past, or of the dead? He said carefully to Greg:

'Hadn't you better be getting over to Gate Thirty-five? It's a fair walk. And you were born on a Wednesday, weren't you?'

'I always thought,' Greg said, 'that it was Thursday's child that has far to go, old man.' He wiped his moustache with his mercurial finger. 'How,' he then said, 'did you know it was Wednesday? *Satu empat jalan.*'

'You can drink on the plane,' Beard said. 'Free.'

'Watch yourself. Be bloody careful. Done my best for you. Well, here's to the dawn flight to Kuching. Coming up like thunder out of. Give us that carol before I go. You know, the Christians Awake one.'

'After that there are no more. That's the lot.' Beard sang softly:

> 'Muslims awake,
> Salute another day
> Of gin *pahits* and Dog's Head stout and B.G.A.
> Great is the law,
> The law the Prophet taught.
> Don't give the bloody thing another thought.
> You're nine hours late for lunch –
> Food grows cold, of course.
> Don't fret:
> Go out and get
> Your tenth divorce.'

'Fratricidal bastards,' Greg said. 'Well, it was nice, old boy old boy. *Selamat tinggal.*'

'*Selamat jalan.*'

Beard watched him go out, took a deep breath, then went over to her.

'Miriam?'

'I remember the Beard part. What's your first name? Lon? Don?'

'Ron. You used to be Sergeant Bloomfield.' Her hair was still black, also curly. Cosmesis probably though now. There was a very slight thickening of the flesh about the chin. But the eyes never changed.

'Ron, yes. Miriam Gillon now, a long time. His first name's Moses, Moishe really.'

'A bit incestuous. And you're on your way to Tel Aviv?'

'From London. El Al. They suspect a fault in the hydraulic something or other, Arabs naturally. They put us down here for an hour. Rome wasn't on the schedule. And you?'

'I sort of, well, live here.'

'With Leonora?'

'You remembered her name better than mine. Why, I wonder? No, she's dead. This year. First day of spring. I think I'm living with a young Italian photographer.'

'A woman?'

'Dear sweet Miriam, I haven't changed all that much. A girl called Paola. She went to Tel Aviv before you, armed with her two cameras. Let's sit over there. If you want to, that is. I mean, you may not want to, that is.'

But she went gracefully ahead of him to the little settle with its low pahit table, negroni in one hand, airline bag in the other. 'Something over twenty years,' she said, seated. 'Isn't it?'

'Now I have to start talking like a television drama,' Beard said. 'The years melt and so on. And time's been good to you.'

'How do you know?'

'Beautiful, I mean, you still, very. That *still* is stupid, sorry, cross it out. But beautiful, yes. Strange, you've been in my head a lot lately.'

'In your head?'

He blushed, Holofernes. 'Thinking of you, I mean. When Leonora died, she died of cirrhosis, by the way, it was then, or shortly after. Lonely, of course, I remembered so much, summer of forty-six and so on. You. That Western Command course I came to give the lectures on. How to run a forces radio station and all that nonsense.'

'It wasn't nonsense. I stayed with that, you know, steam radio as they call it now. Bush House, BBC Overseas.'

'But I came there to give a talk. When that Brunei revolution started. I'd been in Brunei, you see, doing radio. We could have met, we always could have met.'

She flared her nostrils, gently, rhythmically. She had always done, that, a mere habit. He saw her very clearly doing it naked, naked then. What was she like now naked? 'Are you going to Tel Aviv for the BBC?'

'No, for Israel.' She smiled. 'I'm a daughter of Israel after all. Public relations for another Moses, Moishe. Dayan, I mean. It's bad out there. Bombs dropping on Jerusalem. Russian tanks in the desert.'

'Atheistical bastards,' Beard said, and then: 'If I forget thee, O Jerusalem, let my right hand lose her cunning.'

'Don't be silly. This isn't the King James Bible, this is reality.' The voice was huskier than it had been: the excessive smoking of the harassed radio woman. She lighted herself a Marlboro. Then: 'Funny me getting into your head, as you put it, or not so. All you were doing was going back to the past. Why couldn't you go back to her, not me?'

'Back to Leonora? But there was an intermediary, you see. Paola. Paola's about thirty. She sent me back to you.'

'Oh my God.' She coughed and started to wave irritably away the issuing cigarette smoke. 'Men, I'll never understand men. Your wife dies and some little chicky comes along and kindly leads you into the future.' He frowned, not liking this new idiom of hers that had chickies in it. 'But men don't really like live women. They move about too much, they have needs and ideas of their own. There's a character in Aldous Huxley, *Eyeless in Gaza*, who masturbates on his dead wife's underclothes. That's all men, really.'

'That's not quite right. He just kisses them and sniffs at

them or something. You mean necrophily. That's not fair. I don't want the dead, I've shut Leonora out, completely, I'm trying to live again.'

'You mean it's me you want?' He didn't like this either, this mocking directness, she had not used to be like that at all. 'Or just a body you remembered as rather a nice body, and one that didn't want too much of its own way? Leonora too had rather a nice body, a very nice body.'

'How do you know?'

'You couldn't resist showing me pictures of her, as if to say: look, I have this one, and she's a bit of all right, but it's you I'm after now. And she came to that open-air tea-fight we had at the end of the course. I remember well enough. Women do remember.'

'So you remember,' he said, 'us? Everything? No, no, don't say anything about it, I don't care what it was like for you, but for me it was a wonder, a grace.'

'The Marquis de Sade could have said that too, but he belonged to the age of reason. Sorry, I shouldn't tease you. It was good, yes, it was a bit juvenile but it was good.'

'It had to be a bit juvenile.'

'But now you're fifty and I'm forty-three. They have a tiny little hotel in this airport, more like a doss-house really. Shouldn't you be saying: dear Miriam, let us have thirty minutes together on a bed in there, to see how things are now, and then you go off to war and I go back to whatever it is I go back to? Would you like that, Lon or Don dear?'

'It's Ron, Ronald.' He pouted sulkily.

'You'd find some changes, of course. Bodies don't stay still. Pectoral scars. The left breast missing.'

'No,' he said, shocked. 'Darling. I see. Things haven't gone all that — I see. How do you know, you said. One never knows. We judge by appearances merely. I'm very very sorry.'

'Oh, it's not too bad. You feel lopsided at first, then you have to get padding of just the right weight. I'd thought of a silicone injection but then I heard of somebody, some film star I think, getting it in the bloodstream and dying. I'm dying, you know.'

'Eh?'

'Oh, I know we're all dying, but we don't all know what we're dying of, except life, as they say. I do know. Chop a bit off here and a bit off there, but you can't quell the big pulsing thing underneath. That's life too, that thing. You've got to admire it in a way, so determined to live. I started reading Rabelais recently, and Rabelais's rather like that thing – horrible and obscene and intricate and shapeless but so much alive. With a bit of luck I'll beat it though. I want our war to go on just long enough. Daughter of Israel falls, but not of cancer of the rectum.'

There was, of course, nothing for Beard to say, so he said nothing for a moment. Then he said: 'Cirrhosis isn't too bad a thing to die of.'

'Have you ever died of it?' she said bitterly.

'Sorry. Sorry sorry sorry. Let me get you another of those. A negroni?'

When he had brought it from the bar, and a gin and tonic, the gin being Bosford's, an inferior gin but not one, in his present state, he had the strength to reject, she said: 'So you've been dreaming of my sweet white young body. Touching, pathetic, perhaps even flattering. Go on dreaming of it if you want.'

'More than dreaming. Invoking. It's a kind of rape, I suppose. But the word *love* comes into the fantasy. We used to use that word, remember. I meant it. And I still have to mean it. Because it never had a chance to die.'

'Interesting. My husband would be interested in all this. He's a linguistic philosopher. You love what I was – present tense married to past tense, an impossible marriage. It doesn't at all mean the only kind of love that has meaning – the one contained in *I love you*, I mean. And how about Leonora? You invoke past me – *invoke* was the word, wasn't it? – but never invoke past her?'

'It's never possible to separate the one that got cirrhosis from the one who was all honey and milk and fire and so on. A continuum. Leonora's finished. I dream about her, of course, dream she's back from the dead, but it's always as the enemy, the interferer.'

'The one who interferes with your going back to the past, the past when she was sweet and white and all the rest of it? You're in rather a bad way, Mr Beard. A worse way than me. I've merely got to die. You have to live.'

'Whether I live depends on that girl with the cameras in the Sinai or wherever she is.'

'Yes,' bitterly again. 'One of the neutrals. I'm going to die but I'm also going to live more than either of you. You talk of Leonora the enemy. God, you don't know what the word *enemy* means. What work are you doing now?'

'Well,' Beard mumbled, 'I'm writing a film. About the summer that Byron and Shelley and Mary Shelley spent on the Lake of Geneva. They wrote poems and she wrote *Frankenstein*.'

'What's it about?'

'It's about what I said. They sing songs. And there's a Frankenstein dream ballet. They fall in and out of love with each other. Napoleon's trampling down Europe. The summer ends and they go home. Not Napoleon, of course. Byron and his pals.'

'Oh, my God. Do you want to know what it's really about? It's about men being scared of life. Byron writes about the prisoner of Chillon and Shelley hymns intellectual beauty, God help us, but Mary Shelley sees the reality.'

'You seem to know all about it. What reality?'

'I saw the television thing you did. And I did an overseas radio thing on Mary Shelley. She and her mother are very popular these days. With the forces of women's liberation, that is. It took a woman to make a Frankenstein monster. Evil, cancer, corruption, pollution, the lot. She was the only one of the lot of them who knew about life. That's what it's about, this thing of yours. And what in God's name do you know about life?'

75

'I'm trying to learn.'

'I must go and see about this flight of mine. Don't forget my sweet white body back in forty-six.' She finished her negroni, looked at him thoughtfully, smiled, kissed him gently on the forehead, then left, upright and graceful.

Five

In Geneva Mary and Percy and his limping lordship (come in perhaps on that limp?) looked up at the statue of John Calvin. 'The monster that created a monster,' said Byron, handsomely bitter. 'A clockwork toy called Predestinate Man, wound up by God and arbitrarily set by Him on a path leading to salvation or perdition. No choice in the matter, no freedom in the scheme. How I hate Jack Calvin, how I hate Jack Knox. I was brought up, ye ken,' changing to stage Scotch, 'on the pestilential puritanism of that woman-loather.'

'He preached against the monstrous regiment of women,' Mary said, looking coolly lovely against the background of lake and mountains.

'Regiment meant rule,' Percy said pedantically. 'But Knox has bequeathed us all unknowing an image of women on the march, bugle-blowing, drum-thumping. On the march, though, to what?'

'Rationality,' Mary said. 'Justice, love. The dethroning of the monster.'

'Let us go,' said Byron, yawning, 'in search of some hock and seltzer. I have a damnable thirst on me.'

Beard sat back on his chair in the kitchen. The typewriter, set as it was on the shelves he had placed across the sink, was a little too high for comfort, even though he had cushioned the chair with the newspapers and magazines that Gregson had bought for him. The taps dripped. He had been drinking steadily but now needed food, and he doubted that it would be safe to leave this apartment just yet to get it. Coming back by taxi from Fiumicino, he had had to be dropped on the Viale, since all streets leading to the Piazza Santa Cecilia therefrom seemed to be blocked. He discovered why: a Fascist—Communist confrontation round about the Via della Luce, and a fashionable Christian Democrat wedding in the Basilica of Santa Cecilia. Cars, crowds, police. Beard thanked God for the police when he saw, in front of his apartment block, the trounced *scippatori* of that morning with friends, some of them longlimbed Roman girls, not at all ducklike. The original two snarled when they saw Beard, though it was clearly Gregson they were after. Beard, entering, had slammed the *portone* shut. He hoped that other dwellers in the block, having keyed it open, would also slam it shut. He didn't want any trouble, having had quite enough so far.

'A dish of tea would do very well,' Mary Shelley said. It would too, very strong. Beard went into the front room and looked down on the piazza, which had now shed its wedding crowds and police. They were there still, *scippatori* and friends and girl friends, lounging by the locked gates of the basilica garden, cherubs writhing high above them. Beard had not switched on the light in the front room: they could not see that he was there, looking down on them. They seemed content to wait for whatever they had in mind. One of the boys flipped guitar strings to vie feebly with the mandolin, trumpet, sousaphone and mixed vocal duet that were going the rounds of the diners at Da Meo Patacca. He knew two chords only, but there were enough to accompany the obscene song they trilled, a kind of sub-Belli, in which generalized protest was wound round the genitals of God and His Holy Mother. The girls knew the song as well as the boys did.

The telephone rang. Without too much fear, Beard lay down on the floor to answer it. He had lost hope of this ever being Paola from Israel. If it was Leonora, he was curious to know what tape of her voice in jest or play had now come out of the Hammersmith archives. She would not, he was quite sure, give him a Brunei Christmas carol.

'Mr Beard? Mr Ronald Beard? This is London.' Not too much frying tonight.

'If it's Mrs Beard, please put her on.'

Here she was, but talking, not reciting. It was a very competent imitation of her voice, sharp and not unrefined, with the vowels and tonal variety of a woman brought up in Monmouthshire. 'Darling,' she said. 'I ought to be very cross with you really.'

'I *am* very cross,' he said calmly. 'What *is* your name, by the way – Dymphna? Deirdre? Have we ever met? Are you an aspiring young actress by any chance? And what have I done to annoy you, apart perhaps from writing television plays you wanted to appear in but didn't?'

'Yes,' she said, 'I know it must be hard to take it all in, darling. You thought you saw me die. You assisted at a funeral. But doctors and officials and people make mistakes, you know, so much red tape and inefficiency these days. Anyway, let's forget about the mistakes and you running off to America and Rome and so on. I've had a good long rest. I'm a lot better.'

'What have you been doing for money?'

'Yes, that's all going to be a nuisance, isn't it, persuading banks and the death-duties people that I'm still alive. I had some traveller's cheques, though. Left over from our trip, remember. They were in my handbag.'

'No, they weren't.'

'*My* handbag, darling. The one that went with me when I was moved to the recovery ward. The things that you were told were mine and took away with you were not mine, but you wouldn't know that. Men are very unobservant really.'

'You're doing this awfully well, Dymphna or Augusta.'

The anger that followed shook Beard, it sounded so much like anger well known and remembered. 'Will you get it into your thick bloody stupid fucking head that I'm not Dymph whatever it is or any of your bloody stupid girl friends. This is your wife speaking, do you hear, that was lost and is now found again, and the name is Leonora Beard, née Pritchard.'

'Leonora is dead,' Beard said, shaken but fascinated.

'What you mean is that you want Leonora dead. You want

to start fucking about with nymphs and nereids or whatever they're fucking called. Glad to be rid of your wife, is that it?'

'It's not a question of being glad or sorry, it's just a question of death and adjustment to death and no possibility of adjustment to resurrection.' Script dialogue, that was what it was. 'I can't go back, nobody can go back.'

'No question of going back, stupid. I've been away ill and had a nasty big operation on the National Health and now I'm all right. For a time, that is. Patched up for a time, call it. They give me another six months or so.'

'And then?'

'Irreversible hepatic failure or some such bloody thing. But we'll have six months together, darling, you and I, carrying on where we left off.'

'Drinking?'

'Why not drinking? Nothing to lose now. Besides, we might have an air crash going back from Rome, Arab sabotage or Israeli sabotage or whatever, and there's always the chance of a car accident or food poisoning or choking on an olive at a cocktail party. The rags of time, remember? John Donne? Hours and weeks are but the rags of –'

'And if I say I've other commitments now? If I say I love somebody else?'

'Yes, I heard all about that from the Trenchmores, running off with some little Italian bit.'

'Bint, did you say bint?'

'Bint, if you like, Eyetie bint if you like. You might have waited.'

'I was lonely. Still am lonely.'

'Ah, gone off already, has she? Never mind, darling, you won't be lonely now, I'll see to that.'

'You said something about coming back from Rome. Does that mean you propose coming to Rome?'

'Tonight. I'm fit enough to travel now. Get out of wherever you are, some ratty buggy little flat I suppose, and book in at the Grand or somewhere nice. Double bedroom, double bed.

It's a long time since we had a bit of real love. Then back to London.'

'The Trenchmores are there.'

'They're going to America. Trenchmore's doing the music for a musical. The Hammersmith place will be ours again. You gave away all my clothes, idiot. I must see about getting a new wardrobe in Rome. Everything's going to be all right, you'll see.'

'For six months.'

'Perhaps less. Rags of time.'

Beard breathed deeply for a second or two. 'I don't get this,' he said then. 'I don't get this at all.'

'What don't you get, darling?'

'Look, whoever you are, this is too damned serious and, yes, tragic a matter to make a practical joke out of. Let me congratulate you on the performance, excellent, really brilliant, and then beg you to tell me please what's going on there. Why all this, why? What harm have I ever done you, whoever you are?'

'Now it's you who are joking, darling, but it's not very funny, you know. You never were very funny. That comic series you did for ATV was painful. No wonder they had to stop it halfway. Listen carefully, you slow-witted idiot, sorry, that's what do you call it tautologous or whatever the fucking word is, listen. I'm alive and lucky to be alive, and I hope you think yourself lucky too. A bit like Lazarus, isn't it? Lazara. The Gospel doesn't say how long Lazarus lived after J. C. brought him back, does it? Take what you can, I say. I'm ringing off now. The plane leaves in an hour or so. The airport's almost next door, though. Don't bother to meet me, by the way. I'll get a cab, too late for the Grand tonight I suppose, spend the remains of the *notte* with you and the bugs.'

'Where exactly are you?'

'With Ceridwen. In Manchester. Just outside, actually. Not far from Ringway.'

'Who the hell's Ceridwen?'

'My cousin, idiot. Don't you remember *anything*? Oh, by the way, in your copy of *Vogue* all this business is put rather clearly, death and resurrection and so forth, have a look at it. Can't remember the title of the thing, but you'll find it.'

'What makes you think I'd have a copy of *Vogue*?'

'Are you mad? You always had a copy of *Vogue*. You said the models' faces gave you ideas for characters. Which, as I said often enough but you've doubtless forgotten, explains the total vacuity of your characters. Chow, *nghariad*.' And that was it.

So it was a conspiracy then between this Ceridwen, whom he could not at all remember, and the Trenchmore girl. And probably Greg Gregson came into it too, quite apart from the unconscious myth level. Motivation? That script head at Warner Brothers had been fierce about motivation. Okay, they do that, but what's their motivation? Well, one thing Beard had learned in a life devoted to popular drama was that motivation, of a rational word-of-one-syllable kind, was an ineluctable property of popular drama but, even there, sometimes turned out to be a mere bone thrown to the dogs of reason, meaning reasons, while the true force behind the seemingly inexplicable action was the really inexplicable purpose, even there. One did not produce fiction, even of the elevated Jamesian kind, in order to explain life but in order to evade life. He went back to the kitchen and examined the pile of periodicals on which he had been sitting. *Time, Newsweek* with Moishe Dayan on the cover, *New Statesman, Variety*. There might be an item there about the forthcoming lensing of the Lake Lovers. There might even be something about P. R. Pathan's shame at his inabiity to produce an adequate film version of one of his own novels, hence mad hatred and jealousy of professional script-writers. Motives were always ten a new penny. Then there was *Vogue*.

In the middle of *Vogue*, protected by hostile leggy model girls, was an article by a man or woman called Leslie Hollander, entitled 'Every Widower Feels Like a Murderer.' Meaning perhaps that every widower was really a murderer, at least in the eyes of the new women's solidarity regiment, and hence had to be pursued to death or, failing death, madness. But the article said something about its being very rare indeed for a husband to want his wife back from the dead, there was always a certain relief, even when the marriage had been idyllic, at the closing of the book. New fresh sex, of course, had a lot to do with it, hot loveless but also guiltless sex, a totally different quiddity from marital love. Men were depraved, alas, and knew they were depraved, fantasying in bed about flat young bellies and firm young breasts while the fat droopy but still adored wife lay physically disregarded, dreams oppressed by household accounts and tomorrow's dinner. The widower's sex could not really be guiltless, the wife having in a sense been put away so that flat belly and firm breasts could now be enjoyed in fact not mere fantasy. The guilt a murderer's guilt. Interesting to note that desire of loving husband for wife to return from grave so unusual that literature, where fantasies become real, deals with it very little. Greek myth of Alcestis, invoked in patently insincere sonnet of John Milton about his dream of late-espoused saint coming back after death in childbed. Better-known myth of Orpheus and Eurydice. Gods really on the side of man who wants new flat firm chicky, since ridiculous and cruel trick of Orpheus not being able to look at restored wife if he wants her back impossible of fulfilment to truly loving, and Orpheus is eventually torn to pieces by other women, drunken Bacchantes, for going on burbling about adored and newly lost Eurydice, his head severed floats down river burbling her name. Paradox or anomaly somewhere. True achievement of happy marriage lies perhaps in creation of infinitely subtle and various closed community, private language, a shared history. (Precisely his, Beard's, own point.) What perverse devil in men, not man, men, can see it all end without overmuch regret? Not just a matter perhaps only of sex and f f ch.

A scenario. Man is summoned to hospital, wife dying, hardly

recognizes face of dying wife, accepts it is she, funeral, end, new start, but a big mistake has been made, not wife at all. Wife still alive, recovering from operation in other ward, other hospital indeed. Man finds out later when already, eager, men always eager, committed to new life. Compare stories of airmen, soldiers, missing presumed dead, actually still alive coming back. Story of Enoch Arden, heroic sacrifice, let her be happy with new love, off into night, impossible melodrama. Law and logic and love demand gladness, rejoicing, that happy marriage not a mere book between covers but a true history to be resumed, only true death ultimately to quell.

So, concluded Beard, that's where they'd got it from, the conspirators. But how far were they going to be willing to take the cruel fabrication? Surely not to the extent of someone in the guise of resurrected Leonora actually flying out here to Rome? A laughing vicious dénouement, the joke revealed as a joke: was this worth the expenditure of good, though recently devalued, pounds sterling on an airfare? It had all been worked out, though, highly plausible. There was a great international airport at Ringway, outside Manchester, and there would undoubtedly be a night flight to Rome, via Milan, the Italian Manchester, therefrom. What Beard had to do now, it seemed, was to get away from here, but would that thwart the joke or fulfil it? And would not getting away from here, meaning leaving this apartment and finding some dim *albergo* off, say, the Via Nazionale, be a sort of admission that his relationship with Paola was not after all to be pursued? Not necessarily, an apartment was only an apartment, especially when it was empty as this one: a matter of a note sent to the *Mondiale*, awaiting her return, explaining all; each day spent in telephoning this number here, in case of her sudden return. Another question, not now to be seriously put; was the true aim of the conspiracy, in which Pathan also would have to be implicated, the quelling of his *vita nuova*, apt Dantesque term, with dear sweet desirable Paola, and if so why? But, expert in motivation, he knew it was pointless to ask why.

Still, travelling light as he was since the first day of spring, making a swift getaway was no problem. He had a small plastic bag or grip drooping from the handle of the door of *lo studio* and, on a hanger hanging from a nail on that same door, two drip-dry shirts, three ties, his suit, his present garb being working garb. The repossessors had either not noticed or, more likely, creating a quick instinctive *gestalt* between those things and the script in progress, not been interested. Making a getaway must, he felt, be left to impulse, not be planned. The psuedo-Leonora, if coming at all, would just now be about arriving at Ringway Rirport. He went back to the front room, looked out and saw that the *scippatori* and friends were no longer lounging by the basilica gate, nodded without satisfaction since he had known that they must eventually tire, switched on the light and fed his eyes with Paola's oblique Rome. Then he looked up a number in his small black book and carefully dialled. To his surprise he got the number immediately.

'Trenchmore here.'

'Incredible, never thought I'd be able to dial it right first time off, all this arithmetic and then one's own number shy in strange company at the end.'

'That sounds like Ron Beard, complete with TV dialogue. Been trying to get you all day but no luck, lucky you rang. Look, urgent, I don't need the house any more, it's work, you know all about work, you're in the same racket yourself, a matter of crossing the water. You won't insist on being paid for the whole three months, will you? Are you there, can you hear me?'

'Yes. You're going to do the music for a musical. Leonora told me. It's not *The Lovers of the Lake*, by any chance?'

'No, very wet that sounds, oh it's yours, isn't it, sorry, but it's still a lousy title, no, this is ballet music for something about Frankenstein, interesting idea. Leonora? Leonora? Leonora couldn't have known, man. It's only just come up.'

'All right, you don't have to pay, just leave the key next

door, no need to move the piano till you're ready, listen. What's the name of your eldest daughter? How old is she? Is she fond of practical jokes? Is she what you'd call a malicious girl?'

'Christ, don't want to marry her, do you? She's fifteen and she's named Kathleen and she's going through the serious stage at the moment. Malicious? Malicious? Doesn't like me much now, if that comes under the heading. For reasons there's no need to go into, not unless you're vitally interested. Does that answer your questions and why do you ask them anyway, if I may make so bold as to ask?'

Beard sighed over the long line to London. 'It doesn't matter. Is she with you at the moment? Or is she staying with somebody in Manchester?'

'She's very much here, in bed, or was last time I looked. Friends in Manchester? Why should she have friends in Manchester?'

Beard at that moment heard a loud trolling song from deep down the stairwell. It was a fat man called Alessandrone coming back home from some undefined job: he enjoyed the sound his voice made in the huge sounding-box of the stairwell. 'Well,' he said to Trenchmore, 'that's about all, then. Sorry to disturb you so late.'

'Only too pleased. Glad we've sorted that business out. And don't take this amiss, but I'd say you were a bit old for Kathleen.'

'I seem to be married already,' Beard said. 'Still married, I mean. Christ.' He heard his doorbell burr and a female voice, Italian voice, Paola's voice say something with *darling* in it. 'She's back. She's here.'

'What was that about mar?'

Beard replaced the receiver, scrambled up from the floor. He ran, stumbling, to open up, trying out words like *tesoro mio and amore*. 'Amore,' he said, the door wide open, not one girl but four standing there, though not for long. They were suddenly in, one of them, the tallest, preventing his egress by flattening herself against the now slammed door. Symbolic only, signifying that he would soon enough desire egress when he knew what they intended, and he confusedly knew already. The tallest said:

'I'm American, so there won't be any language problem. Not that there'll be any need for language. Sublinguistic activity, let's call it.'

'You're a student? Who are these?' Not that the question was necessary, since they proclaimed in dress, demeanour, hairstyle or lack of it, their membership of the new international sorority of unchained youth, female chapter.

'I'm not sure that we need onomastics either, but I'm Arlene and that's Donatella, nice name, wish I had it, and that's Maria and that's Paola.'

'*Who?*'

'Paola, feminine of Paolo, which is Italian for Paul. Not a good name for a girl, is it, when you think of Saint Paul and what he thought the place of women was, and better to marry than burn.'

'So,' Beard said, trying to smile but panting hard, 'I know who you are. Now why are you here and what do you want?'

'A matter of vendetta you could call it, two male friends of ours being very annoyed with you but having an appointment to rob an apartment somewhere. Jesus, there's nothing much to rob here. That would have been a laugh, forcing their way in and seeing this. Simple life, is that it? Stripped down to necessities. Necessities? Not many of those, far as I can see.'

'*Arlina,*' said Donatella, who was bronze-haired and might be ultimately Venetian, '*cominciamo. Parli troppo.*'

'Yes, I do, I guess,' Arlene said. 'Strip down to necessities, right.' And she led the way in stripping off sweater and jeans, nothing at all beneath. The girl called Paola, sallow and fattish, giggled when she had pulled all off, insufficiently emancipated. Eight nipples, coming lazily to rest after the brief agitation of undressing, looked at Beard. He said, bravely, looking back:

'One girl, wholly charming, even if she happens to be too

much of a pasta lover, like this one here – Paola, you say, *una desecrazione*. Two, quite acceptable, especially if lesbically inclined. Four, you must admit, miss, you're a scholar, totally grotesque. All those breasts, all that thigh – *troppo*.'

'*Che dice?*' the one called Maria asked Arlene.

'*Niente*,' she said. 'Glad you used that word *grotesque*,' she told Beard, 'mister. *Adesso*,' she told the other girls. They took Beard's clothes off very roughly and, with each several garment, fell into not ungraceful ballet postures, despite the slap of bare feet and the swing and wobble of flesh, as they pulled and ripped. Beginning in the hallway, they were not sure at first whether to overflow into the front room or the bedroom, plenty of room in both. The front room had it, the window being conveniently wide open for the throwing out into the *piazza* of the poor rent bits of cloth – sundered sleeves, single trouser-legs, shirt-rags that the night wind buoyed up briefly, the halves of the armless jacket. 'There,' she said, 'look at that *uccellino*. Shrinking, very fearful. As for the whole body, I'd say forty, fifty, something like that, *old* anyway. But it can be used. You like to put some more clothes on?'

'I haven't any more,' Beard said, covering his genitals with his left hand.

'You must have. *Cercate, ragazze, altri vestiti.*' The three Roman girls flapped and swung about, looking. They found his suit and shirts behind the door in *lo studio* and had a great time ripping and jettisoning those, giggling and downright laughing as, on a too strong two-way rip, they nearly lost balance. 'You find something exciting about this destruction,' Arlene said, studiously studying what he could not wholly hide. He dashed for the telephone, he could at least dial, no he couldn't, didn't know the number, to the window then, at least yell '*Polizia*,' but Arlene neatly tripping him sent him heavily down on to the hard cold travertine.

'Bitch, bloody fucking bitch.'

'Naughty, dirty,' Arlene said. 'Cacophones. Come, lamby-pie, time for the *spettacolo. Una sedia*,' she said to Donatella, who had an interesting collection of moles on her left shoulder-blade. Donatella, a southpaw, animated this while lifting the one remaining chair from the front room, the other now being in the kitchen. Beard was led into the bedroom, Donatella placed the chair with deliberation at what could still, essentially, be called the bed-foot. She courtlily indicated that Beard sit. Beard sat. What he now witnessed he was quite willing to witness; he knew about it theoretically and had even seen photographs, but the fleshly experience, complete with noise and odour, was new to him. Girls working away at each other, the crass purposes of Mother, or Father, Nature by-passed, procuring adequate ecstasties. Two, three, enlaced and rhythmical, but not four, since one, rightly mistrustful of him, always had to stay on watch. Though what the hell he could do about all this was not now clear, and even to report it to the Questura required a vocabulary on his, and a sophistication on its part not easily procurable at such short notice. And if he threw their clothes, duly ripped, out of the window? They would dance off naked through the streets, not giving a damn, and rape any pair of *carabinieri* who stopped them.

What would His Holiness, now innocently asleep in his Vatican, or else busily at work on papers which never once had the word *peccatum* or *peccato* in them, think were he here? More important, what would he do? It was really his job to soft-foot the streets of his bishopric, followed by sin-sniffing cardinals disguised as bullers in cokes, looking for such as this, or listening to voices complaining of its happening on the premises. The trouble was it didn't look sinful. The girls were enjoying it too much, their faces grown Teresan, innocently beautiful, their lips parted as for the reception of the blessed wafer. They had perhaps, those three, looked like this at the *prima comugnione*, as the Romans called it. Not Arlene, of course. Arlene was one of the neutrals, corruptive but incorruptible. She was on watch now, watchful of Beard. She said:

'We'll never be free, not entirely. We require penetration and it has to be done by the holofernes, not by some Japanese surrogate.'

'Where did you get that from – that use of Holofernes?'

'Eric Partridge's Slang Dictionary. The point is, though, that we have to be in control of it. You see that? Like now.'

'Ah, no,' Beard said. 'There are some things no man can be made to do.' Then, in deference to the Italian delegates: '*Ci sono cose che nessuno*, or perhaps it ought to be *nessuna persona, puo far fare a un uomo.*'

'You're very wrong,' Arlene said, shaking her locks of dirty corn, a rained-on harvest, 'as you'll see.'

Never too old to learn, Beard thought sadly, as he lay under Arlene and was vigorously used by her. And by Donatella, or was it Maria? The horror was that there was no tenderness induced by each ecstatic convulsion. When it was the turn of Paola he found himself out of control, there being always a limit to what flesh and blood, especially when one is engorged by the other, can stand, operative word. He grasped the girl powerfully, to her powerful surprise and resentment, and deliberately and briefly pumped his seed into her. She beat him with her fists. The other three cheered ironically. He had not intended that, damn and blast it, that had not been at all his, damn everything, intention. '*Non era la mia intenzione,*' he cried, loud and coarse as a Christian Democrat politician, '*non minimamente.*' But of course no Italian politician would ever apologize for anything.

He was now taunted, chiefly in rough Roman, for his detumescent state. 'You've not finished yet,' Arlene told him. 'We're in control, and we have what we want.' Beard began to say again that there were some things, but these damnable creatures had learnt all the brothel devices of stimulation, from a certain Madrid speciality to one he had thought previously only to be in use among the Tamils. 'Enough,' he eventually groaned. '*Basta, basta,* for god's sake.'

'What do you have to drink?' Arlene said. 'A joint, of course, would be too much to ask for.' When he saw her going into the kitchen he was off that mattress swiftly though painfully.

'Take what you like but leave that typewriter alone.'

'An author, are you?' said Arlene, uncorking the dimple Haig. 'No, a script-writer. Well. "Scene 49. Exterior Day. Alpine scenery in gorgeous sunlight. Shelley, ecstatic, is visited by the Hymn to Intellectual Beauty." Well, crap I suppose. No, Shelley was okay, I guess, a sort of primitive feminist. Mary was a saint, though, a great witness. So, a script-writer, well well. Raw gin's bad for you,' she told Donatella. '*Fa male*. See, I told you.' And back to Beard: 'You must have money. Where do you keep it?'

'In the bank.'

'Not many hiding-places here, I'll say that. Well, we'll have Mr Scriptwriter's typewriter. *Prendiamo*,' she told the three, who were frothing beer freely over their nakedness, '*la macchina da scrivere*.'

Beard grabbed an empty beer bottle by its neck and smashed its base against the top of the gas cooker. 'Touch that typewriter,' he said, 'and I permanently impair such small beauty as you have.'

'Well put,' Arlene admitted, 'but a bit old-fashioned. That your specialty, historical screenplays? We can play bloody, too, you know.' She smashed a beer bottle too, not empty. It gushed over Maria, who screamed as if it were already blood. A naked man faced a naked girl, each with a nasty glass weapon. 'Watch your feet, *ragazze*,' Arlene warned. 'This is ridiculous,' Beard said. 'Right,' said Arlene. 'I think you've been punished. I think you're still being punished. No one types on a kitchen sink out of choice.' The telephone rang loud and hollow from the floor in the next room. 'Don't answer it,' she told Beard. 'You answer it,' she told Paola. '*Tu*. All out of here anyway. Too much glass on the floor.'

Paola gave to the telephone a long and rapid and filthy monologue, in which pedication, cunnilingus, fellation as well as straight and normal frotting or sweeping, though performed in filthy *gabinetti*, were presented in a hagiographic context. '*Chi era?*' Arlene wanted to know. '*Non lo so,*' said Paola. '*Parlava inglese.*' The girls began briskly to dress; it was a tough sex, whatever culture or race it was dressed in.

'You realize,' Beard said, 'I want to get out of here and I can't get out of here. I can't walk the bloody streets naked.'

'You'll find a way,' Arlene said, when her hair had crackled and danced out of her donned sweater. 'What are those photos? Suggested *mises en scène* for that Shelley crap you're doing? They all look like Rome to me. Tut tut, a naked old man confronting four girls decently nay demurely clothed. You should be ashamed of yourself. Christ, don't say it's those pictures that are giving you a hard-on. Some people's states never cease to amaze me.'

'Leave them,' cried Beard, as Maria and Donatella began wantonly to pull the pictures off the walls and tear each one in two. 'No, do it if you want to. I'm past caring.'

Arelene nodded at him. She had, he was able to notice now, rather fine green eyes. 'It's a hell of a hard world,' she said, 'as you may have noticed. Come on, *ragazze. Andiamo. Moviamoci.*' Maria tried to kick his shins with her hard little shoes, but he dodged. Donatella made a tweaking gesture at his shrunken manhood. Paola just giggled. Arlene said: 'I'll tell our male friends to lay off. Consider yourself immune from further visitations.' He heard them go loudly down the stairs, loudly banging on people's doors as they went. He watched them from the window as they turned into the Via Santa Cecilia. Flat-bellied firm-breasted little chickies. He had a sudden great longing for some roast Welsh lamb, mint sauce, and *potch*.

Six

Beard sat naked on the floor and picked up the telephone. He did not dial any number; he spoke to the soft expectant rhythmical purr. He said: 'It's easier for me to address you as Leonora, since I don't know your real name. It's even easy for me to believe that you *are* Leonora. You sounded like her, you even knew the things that Leonora knew, like my getting ideas for characters from the faces of the models in *Vogue*. This is Sherlock Holmes stuff really, I suppose – when all other explanations fail, the remaining one, however bizarre, has to be the acceptable one. So you're still alive, and you're on your way to Rome. All things conspire to the failure of the new life that but two days ago seemed possible. I can't even run away from you. I'm stuck here, bare of everything except my horrible script, my typewriter, and the traveller's cheques zipped up in my typewriter case. I have a raincoat, too tough for tearing, but I cannot seek a hotel at this hour, naked except for a raincoat. Besides, men naked except for a raincoat are common fodder for the prowling police. I have to stay here. I have to suppose that, in about an hour's time, you will arrive at Fiumicino and take the long taxi-ride to Trastevere. When I have finished speaking to you now I shall stoically resume my work, such as it is, and not be surprised when I hear your voice from below, calling for me to open the *portone* and let you in. What then shall I do?

'I can lean out, covered in a bedsheet like an antique Roman, and tell you that you're not coming in, that it's all over, that there was no mistake at the hospital, that Leonora Beard is truly, as well as officially, dead, and that you are a ghost or an impostor. Alternatively, impelled by my loneliness and hopelessness, I can go down, in my shoes and ghostly toga, let you in, carry your luggage up these killing stairs, saying no word, having you behind me Eurydice-like, not looking until you reach these naked lights of this naked flat. Then I shall look at you as coldly as I can, though panting. You will be panting worse, you never could stand even the shallowest climb. I will decide, looking at you panting, whether or not you are Leonora. I know Leonora, you see. I have had over twenty-six years of knowing her. There is a minute mole on Leonora's left cheek, three-quarters of an inch under the eye. The hair-formation known as a widow's peak, fine irony, is very rare, and Leonora has it. Leonora always took size three in shoes. If I insist on looking further, I shall find below the abdomen of the real Leonora a pale almost invisible scar, memento of an adolescent appendicitis operation. If you satisfy my eye and my ear with absolute thoroughness, I shall reject all further doubts. You will be Leonora. Restored. For a brief time, you told me, but all times are brief.

'We shall kiss, but without passion. The restoration will be of the companionate marriage we knew those last years in London. But you will say it was sour grapes on your part; that I denied your right to physical love, and you accepted the denial, but only outwardly. You will indulge, the resurrection being so brief, in certain passionate and urgent assertions – that I denied you physical love knowing full well that you would seek a certain sure outlet for your frustration, one that would in time kill you. You may say also that my insistence on taking you to live in the Far East, with all those stresses, physical and moral, that a European woman cannot easily sustain, was the first step in a slow murder uncalculated, but murder none the less. If you want physical love from me, you must gain it by rape. To rape a male is easy enough for a personable woman. But how personable are you now? Does your breath still smell of the complex chemistry of physical dissolution? Your skin too? Have they paunched you, smoothed you, sewn you neatly?

'A night's crying, then, and, at dawn, reconciliation and sleep. Paola will not return to disturb your sleep, and mine: you can be quite sure of that. Then, at nine o'clock, you will have to buy me something to wear on the Viale di Trastevere. You know my various sizes. Then I can say good-bye forever to this poor stripped flat with its torn views of Rome, locking it and giving the key to the old woman who lives in the flat next door. We book in at the Grand or the Excelsior or the Hilton, and we start to drink. We drink all over a Rome to which the sun has been restored, the rains over and gone, and reminisce as we drink. We shall be content, holding hands, saying *darling it's so good we're back together again*, remembering our first meeting when you were a second-year student and I in my final year, the Spanish Civil War, Munich, our summer wandering France the very year war came. Remember Haines, Betty Pierce-Jones, Valerie Pickering, Punch Williams, the twins from Nairobi, John A and John B, the refectory menu that had Fried God in Batter and the professor of divinity who said he preferred his God plain, Albertine Gosport who smelt of almonds, Jack Pickford who played "Two Sleepy People" and "Skylark", Roy Wright who wrote sub-Rupert Brooke for the magazine and was always messily sick in the Union bar on dance-nights? And the war, and leave, and us hugging each other in that narrow bed in South Kensington when the bombs fell a street away, the joy in finding a man who sold fresh eggs off the ration? I could go on, the good times in the East, forgetting the screaming rows and the discovered infidelities, more than anything remembering the mutual understanding of micrometric nuances of speech and gesture, all restored.

'And we shall return to the house in Clamoursmith, as you called it, and I'll work quietly and you'll read quietly, getting up from your special chair by the electric fire to fry cod deliciously, bring out of the oven a brown pie with marvellous crust, and then the pubs and the games of dominoes and getting ready for Christmas and once you did a tape of the scurrilous carols I wrote in Brunei and your sister in Bedwellty visited us and liked those carols and borrowed the tape and never returned it. Then one day, towards the end of winter, you will retch and say you don't feel at all well and I'll call the doctor and then – It will all lead again to my sitting naked on the floor in a Roman apartment and saying words like these.

'No. Good things become bad things when they are lived through again. There's no going back. As for death, death is the state you're in when people think you are dead. It's no good screeching about official errors and I'm still alive, look, feel. We need death as I need to write THE END on the script I'm writing. Go and be alive to someone else, but not to me. Nothing, however good, must be allowed to go on too long. I've had enough. Let me tell you another thing, Leonora or pseudo-Leonora. You're a liar. You never spoke to Trenchmore about anything. And all this makes me suspect that this is still a hoax, however far you push it. I'm going back to work now, and I'm going to drink while I'm working, and if I pass out while I'm working and fail to hear your noises of arrival, then I shan't have to feel any guilt. Everything's on my side. I'm clean, stripped, used. My stripped arse is cold. End of message.'

Beard went to the bedroom and draped himself in a sheet. Then he went to the kitchen and drank deeply from his bottle of Brandy Stock, putting the fire out with a long draught of Carlsberg. Sighing, he resumed his work. Mary Shelley was on the first few pages of *Frankenstein*, wide-eyed, seeing it all inly, while the thunder cracked over the lake. Byron entered, a little drunk. 'My dear Mary, I've decided against writing a ghost story of my own. Not my dish of tea at all. Your precious husband is out communing with the storm, and you and I are left alone here, save for the servants, who all seem to be drunk, bless them. So I will be out with it at once and say that I adore you. Oh, not intellectually or any of that nonsense of dear Percy's, but in a right true bodily way. I adore your desirable little breasts and the opulent swell of your –' The telephone rang. Beard lay on the front-room travertine in his sheet and picked up the receiver.

'Leonora?'

'What did you say? What was that? Is that Ron Beard? Greg Greg here, old man. Damnable thing happened. Hallo, are you there?'

'Where are you speaking from? The Grand?'

'Wish I were in the bloody Grand, old boy, old boy. No, a damnable thing happened, as I said. We were skyjacked.'

'What?'

'Should have expected it, I suppose, when I got on. When I saw the damn name on the fuselage for that bloody matter. Arabic letters, you know. Four damned armed Israelis on board, confiscated the plane, act of war they called it. Know where we are now? Guess.'

'God knows. Jerusalem?'

'Not quite, old man. Bethlehem. Never thought I'd land up in Bethlehem. Not a bad little place, really, but it's going to be a bit difficult getting to Singapore. Charge the earth here for a gin. Funny me asking you to recite those Brunei Christmas carols. Must have all been working itself out, as they say. They all knew I was going to land up in Bethlehem.'

'Who knew?'

'Whoever's in charge, old man. Whatever organization plans our life's journeys and so on. However, what I really wanted to ring up and tell you was that I saw Leonora again. Here in the hotel, having dinner. So this time I was having no bloody nonsense about being snubbed. I bared the choppers, went up to her as she was spooning in the fruit salad, canned by the way, and said how are things and so on. And she replied in what I took to be Hebrew. So you see anyone can make a mistake. So it perhaps wasn't her after all just by the Dorchester that time. Sorry. This is my second call, by the way, and a hell of a job it is to get through. Bethlehem to Rome – ought to be a clear straight line really. Anyway, your little Eyetie bint was on when I rang up before, and a right bloody mouthful she gave me from the sound of it. I should drop that business if I were you, old man. Won't get anywhere with it.'

'What shall I do then?'

'Oh, take it as it comes. Like me. Here in Bethlehem, the last bloody place in the world I expected to be in tonight, and I've got to get back to Kuching. I'm not worrying. Have a drink, old boy old boy, and let the world slip, as they say.'

'I think I will.'

'Best thing. Must ring off now, costing the earth. I'll report progress. *Selamat.*'

'*Ciao.*'

Greg Greg had cleared him. Leonora was dead all right. Beard took a very large dollop indeed of Brandy Stock, doused the flames with Heineken, then flopped down, in his sheet, in the sheets. He slept heavily but dreamed of a taxi stopping outside in the piazza, someone getting out, crashing at the *portone*, then going away. He woke well, light, purged. Rome was sunny, the morning well advanced. He put on socks, shoes and raincoat. Hairy bare legs shone clearly beneath; would anyone notice? To hell with them if they did. He stuffed his pockets with traveller's cheques and got his passport from his grip. He had two hundred lire in the inside pocket, enough and more for some coffee. In the little bar round the corner nobody seemed to notice the bare legs, but many looked curiously at the raincoat. Fine day, the rain over. He walked, white legs flashing, to the Viale and the Sicilian Bank, where they gave him a good rate of exchange. Everybody looked curiously at the raincoat, taking the legs for granted, eccentric Englishman. He then went to a men's outfitting shop called Bevilacqua. They were astonished at his nakedness and quite understood about the raincoat. Fell among thieves. He bought himself tapering striped *pantaloni*, a kind of striped tarty light pullover, and a waisted blancmange-hued jacket with velvety lapels and hoisted shoulders. All this would do, reasonable working garb. He rejected a hat but accepted handkerchiefs. Now he came to think of it, he had not carried a handkerchief since the first day of spring. Raincoat over arm, pessimistic Englishman, he crossed over to the book-stall facing the poet Belli and bought yesterday's *Times* and today's *Messaggero*. Then he crossed back, sat with a frothy milk coffee at one of the outside tables of the bar next to the Reale, and rested.

The *Messaggero* reported the death and presumed robbery of a woman near the Isola Tiberina. Identification not possible, since means of identification had evidently been stolen with everything else. Woman in early middle age, fair-haired, greying, cracked in back of head with heavy weapon. Police would appreciate help in identification. Tabs in woman's clothes bore name of well-known London women's outfitter. That would do very well, Beard thought, closing the *Messaggero*, pitying the woman. If Leonora had not died heretofore, let this woman be dead Leonora.

The *Times* book page had a review of P. R. Pathan's latest novel, *The Heavens Such Grace*. The plot did not seem to be well managed, the language tended to pretentiousness, the dialogue was remarkably wooden. 'All the characters are alike,' said the reviewer, 'and it is curious to find a taxi-driver using the same modes of speech as the lecturer in anthropology whom he carries. Men, in point of dialogue alone, are undistinguishable from women, and one wonders what precisely Mr Pathan is playing at. There may, of course, be some dark holistic intention of demonstrating that all people are fundamentally the same one person, perhaps the author himself, but novels are made out of the glory of diversity, and there is little here but a uniform greyness. Mr Pathan ought to school himself anew in the essentials of his craft by writing a play, or even a film-script. Lyrical fornication and Turnerian seascapes may be the stuff of limited-edition prose poems, but fiction is action, conflict and, above all, the clash of speech.' Good man that reviewer, never heard of him before.

Beard felt slightly ashamed at not having read the war news first. The war news seemed good for Israel, the Egyptians pushed back to some biblical limit or other. Cease-fire imminent. Blow up the trumpet in the new moon, take a psalm, bring hither the psaltery. Alleluia. Poor Miriam perhaps. Anyway, Paola would be back any day now. His position had become curious, that of an equal, perhaps even a superior. Sex was not, after all, what he had thought it to be: a golden and hardly merited bestowal if one happened to be a middle-aged widower. Beat up a couple of *scippatori* and you at once had an orgy on your hands. Men, who thought themselves the users, had probably always been the used. Paola had better consider coming home to Hammersmith and studying the Penguin book called *Classic British Dishes*. You couldn't fight popes, secular governments and brutal *gallismo* by putting on a Mao uniform and taking pictures of desert slaughter. You had to start building a cosy domestic civilization, best presented to a young woman with Marxist leanings (meaning jargon about superstructures) as complex semiotics.

Beard had lunch in the Rugantino, where they asked for *notizie* about the *signora*. She was bound to be back soon, he told them, and ordered a large mixed grill with chips and please wheel out the Lea and Perrins, having first dusted it. To drink, a bottle of that red Bergerac up on the shelf there. A man came in and forced entertainment on the lunchers, a thick-haired brutal-looking guitarist with a fag-end stuck to his lips. His technique was classical: he played a baroque gavotte and a rococo minuet. When he came round for money Beard gave him three hundred lire and asked him, in very courteous Tuscan, to sit down and have a glass of Bergerac. 'Thanks,' the man said.

'You sound English.'

'I am English. Can you imagine an Italian playing the guitar as well as I play it? They've given a musical terminology to the world, but they're the most unmusical bastards that God ever made. Neapolitan tenors, Christ help us. Verdi and his rum-tum-tum accompaniments. Fault of the language, of course. They always say how musical it is, meaning unmusical, meaning lacking in rhythmical variety, meaning too many rhymes, too few vowel-sounds. Italian is nothing but a Neapolitan tenor.'

'Yet here you are in Italy.'

'There's one man who redeems Italy and it's that top-hatted bugger Belli. You know his work? Blasphemous and scurrilous sonnets. I'm translating them, with the help of the chick I'm shacked up with, as the Yanks put it. I play the guitar for a sort of living, Belli is my real job, not that anybody cares. Do you care?'

'I do, as a matter of fact.' Beard felt both relief and disappointment: that task was being removed from him; he was being freed from that task. 'I thought of translating him myself.'

'Don't,' snarled the guitarist. 'Leave Belli to me.' He struck a six-string chord fiercely – E B E G sharp B E – and bardically recited:

> 'Lot's girls conceived a lech towards their father
>   (Nature's amoral: terms like brutal, nasty
> Don't enter here) and shagged him to a lather
>   Among those caves and rocks, under God's
> vasty
> Sky. God did not speak: it seems He rather
>   Approves of incest, but hates pederasty.

Needs going over a bit,' he concluded, A E A C sharp E.

'Needs going over a lot, excuse me,' Beard said, 'but do carry on. It's valuable work.' B E A crotchet rest D.

When Beard got back to the apartment building he found a telegram in the mailbox. He could not understand it, though he felt sure that it had something to do with the cruel imposture: VICARIOUS REGRETS STOP CHANGE OF LIFE REGARDS HANSON. Who the hell was Hanson and why not the cheaper MENOPAUSE? He went carefully upstairs (who the hell), let himself in (Hanson), then lay on the floor expiring, reading his *Times*. There was an article he had missed, about British film music from Sir Arthur Bliss to a newer slicked generation that included Alfred Trenchmore, winner of Ivor Novello award for his *Blaze of Noon* score, now off to Hollywood to write musical, Michael Lewis, John Barry, others. Who in God's name was Hanson?

At about five o'clock Leonora telephoned, though not from somewhere in Rome, the morgue for instance.

'Such a bloody nuisance, darling, I collapsed in the airport bar, Ringway not Fiumicino, and Ceridwen had to take me back and it looks as if I have to go into a clinic in Cheadle or somewhere. I'm in bed now, not at all the thing, so you'd better pack your bag and be on your way. I need you, need you.'

'What's the address?'

'Dalton Road, Boggartshaw, Number two.'

'Right. Now tell me, do you know anything about anybody called Hanson? Would a telegram saying something about regrets and menopause and signed Hanson mean anything to you at all? Darling, that is?'

'Darling to you, or are you saying darling to me?'

'To you, of course. Darling.'

'The name Hanson means nothing to me. The name Hanson has no more significance than a dried dog turd on the road. It rings no carillons of recognition. Does that answer your question?'

'Thank you. You'd better ring off now and get some rest.'

'Tell me you love me, say you want to hold me in your arms, tell me you'd like to screw me like a rattlesnake. *Say it.*'

This was unseemly desire, ghoulish. Beard gently replaced the receiver. He then gently got down to work and wondered hazily, effect of the Bergerac and the Brandy Stock after, about the origins of the term *kitchen sink drama*.

Three days later Paola returned. He heard a car-door slam in the early hours while he was knotted over his script, a voice that wrung his heart call '*Ciao*' to the departing driver, and he ran to the front-room window to look down on her pushing her key into the *portone*. He swung open the apartment door, flooding light on to the dim stairs, and ran down halfway to greet her.

'*Tesoro mio.*'

'*Amore.*'

She marched upstairs like a soldier, no change of uniform since she had left, knapsack on shoulder, cameras at the alert. He shambled after like a regimental *bishti*, panting, but when she got to the top he jumped ahead clumsily, trying to explain before she saw.

'Don't look. Anything yet. Lot of expl –'

'Anything? There isn't anything to look at.' She sniffed deeply, as for Pathan's special sweat, but took in only, as Beard did himself, a sort of Solzhenitsyn odour of poverty and cheap cigars. 'So,' she said, 'he came. You let him in. I knew you could not be trusted.' She marched from emptiness to emptiness, he following.

'Let me explain, *tesoro*. This man Greg Greg –'

'Who?'

'Gregory Gregson. An old friend, well, sort of, from the East, the Far one, not yours. Passing through Rome on his way back to Kuching. We spent the day together. That gave bloody damnable Prrrrrrp plenty of time to –'

'These seem to be my photographs of Rome. Why did you tear them, why? What has been happening here?'

'Four girls broke in, an act of revenge for what Greg Greg did to those two bloody thieves on a Lambretta, and they were naked and they –'

'Yes, I see. A lot has been happening. Why are you wearing those clothes?'

'When they stripped me, you see, very violently, then I had nothing. Everything out of the window.'

'You were naked too?'

'I had to be. They made me. A terrible time. But I worked really hard at the script, look.' He motioned that she should accompany him to the kitchen. She would not.

'Everything. He took everything. It must have taken him a whole day to do that.'

'Well, I was at the Grand Hotel for a whole day. But I was back in time to see him put the final ashtray in his pocket.'

'You saw him? You spoke to him?' Very eager, no woman could ever really bear to see a man go, especially a husband.

'I played bloody hell with him, or tried to. Those stairs are a bit enervating, you know.'

'Did he speak of any one particular thing?'

'Well, no. Except that you let him down cruelly and were a bitch and might at that very moment of his saying it be sleeping with a syphilitic Arab.'

'Of his saying what?'

'That you were a bitch and unfaithful.'

'I see. He always hated Arabs because they were Musulmans. He called himself a Hindu but he hated vegetables. And he hated black men very much.'

'I got vicious with him, naturally. I mean, there's no need for me to mention that, is there?' Beard, now well equipped with breath again, lighted a Mercator.

'You must stop smoking those things. You will not be able to afford it.'

'Oh, I can afford them all right,' Beard said cheerfully. 'Now, *amore*, tell me all about the war.'

'It was photographs he was looking for. It was easier for him to take everything away. He would think the photographs would be hidden somewhere. But the photographs are in the Banca Commerciale.'

'What photographs?'

'Photographs of him,' she said calmly. 'Doing the things he would insist to do. Here in this apartment.'

'Sexual things?'

'I suppose they could be called sexual things, but very dirty. I took pictures of him. I thought I would use them for for for –'

'Blackmail?' Ah, if those stripped walls could but talk.

'Yes. If he tried to have me put in prison for adultery or

fornication. He would do that. He has said before he would do that. So I needed the the –'

'Blackmail, I see that, yes. Would you like some coffee, *tesoro*? I bought tin mugs and a small pan and Nescafé. We have fire. We have water. We even have somewhere to sleep. Stripped down, like soldiers. What was the war like? Did you get good pictures?'

'Horrible. And so horrible pictures. Which may mean good pictures. Deserted, this apartment. A desert. Well, it may be better so. Less work, anyway.' She began to strip, but coldly, as for a routine free-from-infection. 'No coffee, coffee is not a thing to take like that. Casually. Some of them would give anything for a cup of coffee. And a cigarette. I have given up smoking. We shall need every lira. Take off those horrible clothes and then we will get into the bed. I see, we have no bed. Like the desert. And in bed I will tell you everything.'

'No talk,' he said. 'Love, just love. We'll talk tomorrow.' He tried to embrace her nakedness, but she was stern in rejecting him.

'A different kind of love,' she said. 'It is another kind of love we have to think of.' Oh Christ, Beard thought. What war does to people. At least they were naked together when they got into bed, if it could be called that, but the nakedness seemed to signify deprivation, not promise volupty. It fitted the flat.

'Darling, darling.'

'No, not now. Listen, it was a terrible thing the war, even if it was so short. It is the suffering of the innocent that is so terrible. Now you have a chance to do some proper work.'

'What do you mean, proper work? I've been working like a slave.'

'Can you think of that as real work? Writing a film about silly men writing silly poetry and ignoring all the great wrongs of the world outside them?'

'I'm not having that. I suppose somebody's been telling you how marvellous Mary Shelley was for writing about male tyranny and pollution and Christ knows what all rolled up in

105

the monster Frankenstein. Well, at least Shelley and Byron *did* something. Shelley was a martyr for intellectual liberty and Byron died for Greek independence and dear sweet Mary becomes a great saint for writing a hysterical Gothic sub-novel. You call that justice? My film tells the truth. As far as it can, that is. Did you by any chance meet a woman at Moishe Dayan's headquarters who – Never mind. It doesn't matter.'

'Now I will tell you what does matter. The refugees. The children who have lost their homes and their parents. We are going to have seven of them here. Or it may be eight. I have a list of their names in that bag. So you see it is a blessing in a way that the apartment has been made naked. They are used to sleeping on floors. You will be useful with the language.'

Beard could say nothing for about twenty seconds. 'Refugees?' he then said. 'In here? But the landlord won't allow it.'

'The Pope has given his blessing and so have the Christian Democrats. The Communists too, of course. The landlord can do nothing.'

'Jewish refugees?'

'No, stupid, the Jews have won the war. These are all Arab. They have names like Hassan ibn Abdullah and so on. Isa binte Ismail.'

'Omar Ali Saifuddin?' Beard began to feel lightheaded.

'You know Arab. It will be useful.'

'I don't know Arabic. Except for the few Arabic words that got into Malay. Look, angel, treasure, darling, this is madness.'

'A madness we need. I have been thinking how we can arrange the rooms. We shall have to sleep in *lo studio*, which is the smallest. We may have to have the small *epilettico* in there with us, though. I do not trust the others with him.'

'A small epileptic?'

'Yes. I think he is the one called Omar Ali whatever it was. The eldest girl Isa, which means Jesus, did you know?'

'I knew.'

'She is not very responsible. Perhaps her head-sores have

something to do with that. She was badly beaten by somebody. She will lift her skirt up at you. I am not sure if you can be trusted now after the story you told me.'

'I can be trusted. I can very much be trusted.' The thing to do probably was to go out and get very drunk and daub SCREW THE POPE outside the Sistine Chapel. No, too many might approve. Or UP FANFANI'S ASS outside the Quirinal. Something, anyway, that would make the police grab him and take him to the Questura building off the Via Nazionale. Refuse to speak Italian, say *Fuck you Eyties* all the time. It would end up with deportation, not my intention, *tesoro*.

'All the people you talk of in Borneo had names like Abdullah and Ismail. You know the Koran, you say. Some of your radio programmes were in Arab.'

'You mean I have to stay here all day and look after epileptic Arabs?'

'Palestinian Arabs. You can write your scripts. We shall need the money. I will go out as before and work. We are trying to make that big empty place down the street into a refugee centre.'

'Who's *we*?'

'The Roman Press Association. You cannot conceive of the horrors of war.'

'I had six years, damn it. This was six days. I refuse.'

'You talk of loving me. It is just my body you want.'

Beard took several deep breaths. 'Let's talk about all this in the morning.'

'It is morning now.'

'When the sun rises. When we've had some Nescafé.' The telephone rang. 'Ignore it,' Beard said. 'It'll be Greg Greg again. He's trying to get back to Kuching, but he got skyjacked at Karachi. He'll be in Samarkand now, I should think.' But she got out of bed, if you could call it that, naked. He followed her, naked, sighing. He could do with some Nescafé now. And Brandy Stock, of course. He lighted the gas and put on a cheap battered saucepan with stale water already in it.

'*Pronto.*' And then: 'Yes, I speak English.'

'Told you it was Greg Greg.'

'Yes. I see.' She moved from incredulity very quickly to a kind of horrified interest, then to concern promising outrage. 'Oh yes, terrible, I see. I will, yes. I am very sorry, I did not understand. Yes. Good-bye.' She, denuded, faced Beard, denuded, who had let the flat be denuded, who had himself been denuded, who had allowed denuded girls to denude the walls of so many of her photographs and then tear them, who was unimpressed by the plight of Palestinian Arab refugees, faced him like one shaken, in spite of all before, by the final revelation of turpitude, but calm, as befits one who has seen war in a desert place. 'The name she gave,' she said, 'was Mrs Beard. Your wife. You said your wife was dead.'

'And so she is. Whoever that was, it was an impostor. Said she was dying, did she? Said I must be by her bedside? Damn it, I did all that last March. She's dead, I can prove it. That's been another thing that's been going on while you've been away. Persecution.'

What she said now she said mostly in Italian. He bowed his head as if it were comminatory Church Latin. The rain began to hiss outside, like the chorus in Bach's *St John Passion* demanding crucifixion.

Seven

I

Mrs Ceridwen Beard served a special dinner tonight. The main course was a dish that had once been popular with large South Welsh miners' families on pay-nights: a piece of beef and a small chicken cooked slowly together with leeks, onions, carrots and potatoes in good meat stock, a large glass of port added some way towards the end, a small glass of brandy shortly before serving. The dessert was gooseberry pie and double cream. There was a plate of Welsh-cakes to fill up any odd corners. Being Welsh, she did not much care for the Irish, but she was good at making Irish coffee. They sipped this by the fire, waiting for the film to start. The television news was as bad as ever, full of war in the Holy Land and battered Palestinian refugees. The telephone rang during it.

'It'll be her,' Ceridwen said. 'There's inconsiderate with your film coming on.'

Leonora Beard, or Mrs Gwyneth Hanson, had accomplished two resurrections and was now on her third death.

'Yes?' Beard said to the telephone.

'Darling, I'm dying. They've put me in this small room at the end of the ward. Come and shag me. I want to be shagged before I die.'

'But they're showing my film on television. You know, the one about Frankenstein.'

'Typical of you, you bastard. You think more of Frankenstein than of your poor wife.'

'Try and get some sleep, dear. I'll be round to watch you die when the film's over.'

'Fucking dirty swine. Bigamous bastard. I'll haunt you, you'll see. I'll be hovering over your filthy bed, laughing at your fucking ineptitude.'

'Try and get some sleep, dear. It's starting now.' He rang off.

Trenchmore's music growled loud and fierce during the opening titles. It then suddenly became insincerely lyrical. It crashed and howled to the limit over the names of producer and director. 'There's noisy,' Ceridwen said.

The film was entitled *Milord Lucifer*. It had not done all that well on the circuits and had been quickly sold to television. It totally lacked intellectual beauty, and there was very little of Shelley to be seen or heard. It was all Byron, limping and exopthalmic about Lake Leman, shagging various *contesse* and also Mme de Stael. Mary Shelley, a very full-breasted girl, turned him in revenge into Frankenstein, wanting him but not getting him till the very end, when *Frankenstein* had already been completed and, with impossible speed, published. There were no songs, but atmospheric Trenchmore was always ready to growl and thump or wax insincerely lyrical over décolletaged passion or the Alps, sometimes both together. There was talk about Mary becoming Lady Byron when Shelley, anachronistically shipwrecked amid thunder and lightning, had been briefly but eloquently mourned for, but you could see that nothing would come of it, more free fornication and an eventual Missolonghi shining in Byron's eyes and the lake they brooded into.

Beard had, naturally, seen the film before and had, indeed, assisted with the post-sync work, but he agreed with Marshall McLuhan that televisual framing radically changed the aesthetic impact of a film made for the large screen. 'What a bloody waste,' he said to Ceridwen. 'Will the cinema ever grow up?'

'Not in your lifetime, *cariad*.'

'But perhaps in yours?' He smiled down at her dark lissomness and fondled her neck.

'*Our* life time. Stop thinking about age all the time, idiot.'

110

She was thirty-three and looked about twenty-six. And then: 'What did Gwyneth say this time?'

'The usual. She wants to be laid on her deathbed.'

'A great strong strapping woman like that. She should never have married that Hanson.'

'I didn't know she had, as you know. I'd always thought of her as Gwyneth Isherwood.'

'Both of them weeds.' How clear and monophthongal that high front vowel, positively Mediterranean. 'She should have stuck to acting.'

'She did stick to it. She has stuck to it.'

'I think this act has been going on too long. Incestuous as well as obscene. I'll always answer in future and say you're not in.'

'Funny thing, incest. Nothing to do with blood, really. Mystical you could call it. *He copulated with his late wife's sister.* That sounds terrible, doesn't it?'

'*She copulated with her dead sister's husband.* That sounds worse. I can see how it might turn somebody on, somebody a bit, you know, unbalanced.' It seemed to turn Ceridwen on, or it might have been Paul Newman or Byron, or it might be Beard's hand caressing her neck, shoulders.

'To bed?'

'No, here. I like it in front of the fire. You're putting on a bit there,' she said, fondling his belly.

'You feed me too well.'

'I must feed you less well. And you really must cut down on your smoking. *Diw mawr,* your heart. Racing like mad.'

'That's nothing to do with smoking.'

2

'Genuine freedom,' Beard said, 'for the first time in my life. I can smoke, drink and eat to excess and not give a damn about it.'

He sat smoking his fifth cigar of the morning in Dr Bloomfield's office. It was the sixth of January. There was something vaguely familiar about the picture calendar on Dr Bloomfield's wall. They had the whole morning before them. Thanatology was a comparatively new discipline. Not many sought the services of a psychopomp. Dr Bloomfield had no other appointments till three in the afternoon. The two might even have lunch together, a big one with big brandies and big cigars after, Beard paying.

'That calendar,' Beard said, squinting. His sight was not so good these days, and that was a nuisance. Hardly worth while to go to an ophthalmic specialist. Waste of money. 'It looks familiar, that scene.'

'Views of Rome,' Dr Bloomfield said. 'Rather original that sort of oblique approach. A gift from Tannenbaum's Medical Supplies in Geneva. Now then, how are you feeling?'

'Well. Sight not so good, a slight sense of deadness in the right calf. Appetites unusually powerful, including the sexual one.'

'That's classical, according to MacGregor's report. But how he can know that beats me. Schweitzer's Disease is even less common than Hanbury's. Or Diplock's.'

'How long does he give me?'

'Six months. Three. A lot depends on the care you take of your heart.' Dr Bloomfield looked, far more than himself, Beard thought, like a man who ought to take care of his heart. Only about forty, but an unwholesome roll of white fat had swallowed his neckline hook and sinker. He had a senior prelate's paunch. He smoked unfiltered cigarettes one after the other. Perhaps the look of moribundity was mandatory in a psychopomp; it begot confidence in the patient, suggesting that here was one who would literally lead the way.

'My heart can look after itself,' Beard said. His cigar had gone out; he relighted it.

'Very well. Let's have questions first. Then we'll see what general considerations they lead to.'

'Should I tell my wife?'

'Oh, I can't advise you there. My experience tells me that the patient always tells, sooner or later, even when he's vowed not to. He has a couple of drinks and then sort of boasts about it. Or he uses it as a device for gaining pity when his wife's been making the usual periodic round of his faults. Still, it's an unpleasant thing for a wife to have to live with. And the husband gets jumpy. She keeps watching him, you see. One thing you could do is go away. On business, call it. Then the death's reported – cardiac attack, food poisoning. Some small North African town perhaps, where the hotel call in the police and the police have you buried quickly because of the heat.'

'It would be horrible to go away too soon. Two months living on bad couscous when I could be eating leek broth and Welsh leg of lamb and, well, you know.'

'The comforts of marriage, yes, I see that. Now, according to MacGregor, there's a very sharp signalling device the disease uses, you know, rather like the light flashing a warning about no juice left in the tank. The left eye starts to twitch, always the left apparently. If it's the right it means nothing. Useful language, English, full of mnemonics. Right: all right. Left: not much left.'

'How long does it twitch for?'

'Anything from ten days to a fortnight. You could cover it with a patch to save embarrassment. Then comes coma. Poetical, that. Then comes coma. It's not a bad disease,' Dr Bloomfield said, adding a new link to his smoke-chain. 'I wish to God there were more like it. Cancer's awful. Cancer really makes one believe that evil exists. Cancer is the living body of the *nequissimus draco*. That,' he explained, 'is what the devil is called in the old exorcist's book of words. They don't use Latin any more, worse luck.'

'I thought you were of the Jewish persuasion.'

'I'm anything and everything. I have to be.'

'Miriam beat the dragon.'

'Just about. She got spattered two hours before the cease-fire. A marvellous girl.'

'I agree. How old is Moses or Moishe or whatever he calls himself?'

'About my age. Why?'

'Has he thought of remarrying?'

'No, he pushes on with his linguistic philosophy, whatever that is. But I know what you have in mind. Give him a call sometime. Invite him to dinner. He's not orthodox. He'll eat lobster seethed in its mother's milk. Next question.'

'What happens after death?' Beard had expected Dr Bloomfield to gawp at that and say *oh my dear fellow for God's sake*, but instead he nodded and took a deep puff, obviously used to the question.

'You ask me that,' he said, 'not because you're really, as it were, *positively* interested. You're frightened that there may be a hell, isn't that it? People are all the same: they can do without heaven but they can't do with hell. Now, tell me: what are you feeling guilty about? Why do you think there might be eternal or quasi-eternal punishment awaiting you when Schweitzer's Disease gives you the final knock?'

'I was bad to my first wife. I'm not sure that I'm all that good to my second. There was a girl in between the two that I let down very nastily. What I think I mean is that I've failed in charity, knowingly, deliberately.'

'We all have. But if we don't give one way we can always give another. You've given pleasure to people. There may be a lot of sick lonely people who bless your name, if they know it. You know, films and television and things. Things that have given them a lift.'

'That's a trade. Charity isn't something you get paid for.'

114

'Nobody ever gets paid for *values*. You do your work, and value is an extra bestowal. Value comes when you make a thing better than it need be. As for charity, everybody's limited by his temperament and his vocation. It's no good being guilty because you can't, for instance, give homes to a million war orphans. All right, you could pack five or six in the spare room and throw them a packet of Uncle Ben's rice every day. But that's only charity in the nasty nineteenth-century sense. Charity means *caritas* means love. And the first person you have to learn to love is yourself. Do you love yourself?'

'No.'

'Well, you'll never love anybody. You've a lot of work to do in the next few months, learning self-love. You don't want to go out hating. Start with your left hand, admire its formation, wonder at the mobility of the fingers, give thanks for the thumb, adore the creases of the knuckles. Love the fat on your belly. Listen to recordings of your voice, marvel at the infinitude of tonal variations. Love your appetites.'

'And is the disease part of me? Is this deadness in the right calf something to be loved?'

'Of course not. That's the enemy, but not the lovable one that's also your neighbour. That's the *nequissimus draco*. Fight it through philosophical submission. Of course, it's easy for you. Not so easy if it's cancer. Miriam called in another enemy, she exercised human choice. She, incidentally, went on loving her body. She pitied it too, of course, but there's no pity without love.'

'You realize, of course,' Beard said, 'that you haven't defined love.'

Dr Bloomfield sighed out a great deal of blue smoke. 'Symbiosis,' he said. 'The sense of a single living unity. The desire to be part of it, the desire for a part of you to be a part of it.' Beard shook his head sadly. 'You don't seem convinced,' Dr Bloomfield said. 'But you will be convinced. You *have* to be, damn it.'

3

It was about the time that the twitching began that Beard received his last summons to Rome. Ceridwen remarked on the twitching early. The eyes of a woman, Beard knew, missed nothing.

'Don't worry,' he told her. 'It's probably overwork.'

'If you go about twitching like that in Rome you'll be in trouble. Hot-blooded husbands and so on. I don't think you're well, you know. Is this Roman business very important?'

'It's interesting, that's the main thing. A six-part television serial on the life of Spinoza. A joint Anglo-Italian production. No lack of room for ideas and intellectual dialogue. No room for anything else. I may not do it, of course. I may not care for my Italian collaborators. But I think I ought to go.'

'How long will it take?'

He could have cried at that. 'Not very long. I'll have another Welsh-cake if I may. And some more tea.'

'You *are* getting fat, you know. Oh *Diw mawr*, there she blows. I think we'll have to stop this, you know.' The telephone had started to ring. 'You've been too tolerant. Me too.'

'Call it a penance. For me, I mean.'

'You were good to Leonora. If you were half as good to Leonora as you've been to me, she had no right to be anything but very very happy. Take the thing off the hook. Let her rave and bugger and blast to herself.'

'She ought to be pitied. Which means she ought to be loved.'

'Loved? That thing? When I think what I did for her, having her in my digs in Manchester, and getting all that information from the Trenchmores, and there she was creeping downstairs and being venomous on the telephone. All overseas calls, too. I made her pay, I can tell you.'

'As you've already told me, *tesoro*.'

'What was that word? It sounded Italian.'

'*Cariad*, I should have said. There, she's got tired already.'

The ringing had stopped. 'I'm trying to love her,' he said. 'I'm doing my best to love.'

'You don't have to. It's enough to love me, isn't it?' She put her long white hand on his puffy brownish one. He winced. There was a pain starting there; he must tell MacGregor about that: augment the catalogue of symptoms for future use, if any.

'Enough,' he admitted.

'You look really lecherous with that eye,' she giggled.

He bought an eye-patch at a chemist's on Hammersmith Broadway. When he left for Rome from Heathrow he was frisked with, he thought, more than regular thoroughness by the security guards. A piratical look, the suspicion a hangover from reading children's comics or seeing *Treasure Island* on television. When he arrived at the Grand Hotel he found Greg Greg already there. He was travelling west this time: going on leave, not coming off. They expected each other; Beard had quietly cabled Kuching; Gregson could take his annual leave pretty well when he liked.

'You look like Long John whatsit, old man. What did you do, knock yourself on the corner of the bar when you heeled over?'

'Something like that. What are you drinking?'

'I'll get these, old boy old boy. Gin, *molto* big, a kichey drop of *merah*, tonic, two, *lekas-lekas*.' Beard looked at him, fatter, shinier, and tolerated him, no, loved him. He loved the mercurial finger wiping the thin grey moustache; that whole brown spotty fat hand was a marvel of engineering.

'Haven't see Leonora again, have you?' Beard asked.

'Thought I saw her on Batu Road, Kuala Lumpur. I was up there filling in for old Seymour. Wasn't her, though. Gave me a load of what seemed to be Dutch. No, take your word for it now. She's dead all right. Anyway, there's another Mrs Beard now, isn't there? Cheers, *selemat minum*, may you live forever and me live to bury you.'

'*A proposito*,' Beard said.

'Eh?'

'You ever hear of the Protestant Cemetery?' Beard said. 'Here in Rome?'

'Come off it, old man, this is a big RC town, atheists allowed but no Protestants.'

'Keats is buried there, one whose name was writ in water, also Shelley. There may be room for Ron Beard. Anyway, you're in charge of the body.'

Greg gaped. 'Are you —? What the —? Do you mean to —? Fair's fair, old man, come off it.'

'It's coming any day now,' Beard said fiercely. 'I'm luckier than most. I know it's coming. Damn it, man, I've done better than Shakespeare, Napoleon, a bloody sight better than Marlowe and Keats and, Jesus Christ, Chatterton. Jesus Christ, too,' he added.

Greg Greg was very thoughtful. He gave the next drink order in plain English. 'So,' he said, 'you're going to snuff it. I believe you, old man. No reason for you to lie, nothing in it for you, all said and done. The quacks all agree on it, do they? Can't always trust the buggers, as you know. Funny thing, I'm not very good at death. What I mean is, I find it hard to believe that anybody's actually gone and snuffed it. I keep seeing people, as you know. Like Leonora, one example. I'll keep seeing you, going over in a bar and saying *how is it then*, or at an airport or somewhere, and getting the fish-eye or a mouthful of Lower Slobovian. If I'd lived in old J.C.'s time I'd have had no trouble at all in believing, come to think of it. Lazarus from the grave, I'd be the first to see him in a bar, if they had bars in those days, Jesus bar-Joseph, different thing altogether that. And old J.C. himself, no trouble at all. Who was that doubting bugger?'

'Thomas.'

'That's right. Christ knows how he got the job, being a doubting bastard like that. How do you feel then, old man?'

'As well as can be expected. The sentence ends with a coma, any day now. But I'm not going to wait for it. Beat the bugger, as I hope you'll see. What I want you to do is to arrange things with the Embassy, probably Consulate, the Embassy's only for big things. I don't know whether the dear British government allows foreign currency for burial abroad. They probably say everybody's duty is to die at home now the Empire's gone. Unpatriotic to be buried in Italy. Anyway, it's the Protestant Cemetery I want, if there's any room.'

'I'll bloody well make them make room, old man, if that's the place you want. Kick some of the other sods out. Come on, you're slow. Two gins, *molto* enormous, Jewseppy.'

4

There was no farewell letter for Ceridwen. She had, on marrying him, naturally given up her teaching post in Manchester, but she had kept her District Bank account open. He had silently transferred his own monies to that, thus beating death duties, one in the eye for the inimical State. He did not, however, think that she would suspect anything. Sudden heart attack, no foreknowledge. They did not have any secrets. An act of love, the giving of everything. Even the Hammersmith house was in her name. He would telephone later and say he loved her. His task now, while Greg Greg snored off the afternoon's freight and prepared for the evening, was to write – in pen too, which was very tiring for a professional script-writer – a letter, his first and last, to Paola. He wrote:

'Dearest Paola, *tesoro, amore*, and all the other words. I would like to write in Italian, but I remain at the end a monoglot Englishman, unworthy to enter any comity of nations, tied to one tongue as to one cuisine and one insular complex of myths. But I think if I said now *Domina non sum dignus* it would sum up how I feel. You restored me to life in a bad time and my gratitude knows no end. But writing that I see the falsity of it. I should have shown gratitude by showing willingness to accept a new world, yours, which rejected superficial order, cosiness, smugness, yawning over the fire. I thought I was ready to be stripped naked and indued with a new chivalry, meaning a new charity, but I was too old and too weak and too frightened. I ran back to the known, but was blessed more than I merited with the love of someone who possessed, possesses, your charity and your passion and something of your beauty, as well as belonging to the one world I know. Still, I confess a failure and beg forgiveness. I end by telling you that I love you.'

It would have been so much easier for Beard to imagine a situation in which a dying man wrote a final letter to a loved woman. He could have been eloquent, he knew. He felt sick at the hypocrisy of his craft and the knowledge that words did not work well in the service of truth. He put the letter in an envelope and wrote her name in hotel ink: Paola Lucrezia Belli, family of the beautiful ones. He proposed delivering it tomorrow.

Before reaching a state of slurred speech, Greg Greg, whose name seemed now to have something to do with shepherds and flocks and feeding lambs, expressed himself willing to ring up 581 9345 and find out who was there. He came back to the bar and said:

'That Pathan bastard's there. Could tell from his toffee-nosed accent and having no *r*. You know, *all gwight I'll bgwing her to the fayoon*. Then this bint comes, nice voice, low and sexy, sorry, old man, shouldn't have said that, and I say, posh as I can, that Mr Linklater of the London *Sunday Times* magazine wants to discuss some pictures with her and this is a shocking line, can hardly hear you, may I ring at three to-morrow afternoon. And she says all right and that's it. Done the proper thing, have I?'

'I felt sure she'd still be there,' Beard said. 'Once you've got a flat in Rome you don't move, you wait till the landlord kicks you out. Still, she might have been away, on a job. As for that swine Pathan – well, I don't suppose I'm really surprised. If you're indifferent to a girl you don't steal her underwear. He's a broken reed really, poor bastard. He needs her.'

The following morning Beard took a taxi to the administrative centre of Radiotelevision Italiana, outside whose main entrance a big stone stallion cavorted – the only creature in the entire organization, so it was said, that possessed balls. He had a meeting with Dr Ottavio Cenci, Dr Mario Positano, and Dr Emilia Carlo d'Amico. None of them understood much English, but Beard managed to communicate his situation – major operation coming up, lack of real ability anyway to deal with the project, might he recommend heartily one of his past collaborators, George Halliwell-Stubbs? The surname was listened to with incredulity and taken down approximately. Then Beard went off to have lunch at the Rugantino with Greg Greg, who had a bad hangover. It started to rain. They had antipasto with gin and tonic, a kind of mixed grill with two bottles of Bergerac, and vanilla ices soaked in whisky. Afterwards they had double espressos and Strega.

'I want to,' Beard said, 'get there by way of the,' staggering a little, 'Belli statue. Pay homage.'

'Sure you wouldn't rather go the quick way, down there? You don't look so good, old man, if you don't mind my –'

'I'm all right. Ought to have brought our raincoats really though, I suppose.' They passed the Esperia and the Reale and the empty taxi-stand. 'There he is,' Beard said, 'hater of cant, fighter against religious hypocrisy and secular tyranny.'

'Pity about that top hat, old man. I mean, the head and the hat are carved out of the same blob, and you know bloody well there's no top of the head there. Only that sodding hat.'

'I should have spent more time fighting the State. The Inland Revenue killed Dylan Thomas and Exchange Control allowed George Orwell to die of TB instead of going to a Swiss sanatorium, and, ah Christ, man, you could go on forever. Fuck the State.'

Gregson recited in a finicking accent:

> 'You cannot fuck the Government, alas:
> It's fucking your own image in a glass.
> To think of fucking it's a waste of time:
> Why add good semen to a tub of slime?'

'Who wrote that?' Beard asked, feeling the faintness approaching.

'Well, this one, wasn't it? Belli, no, Bellow, no, Belloc. My old dad used to recite that at us. Hey, watch it, old man.'

Too late. Beard went over, in good ancient Roman style, in front of the statue of a great man. He did not hurt himself. He fell next to a small puddle in a rut and saw, close to, something of Rome reflected. So that was what it had all been about. 'All right,' he said, getting up. 'Not to worry.' A couple of passing women said *ubriaco ubriaco*, and one of them made a swigging gesture. Greg was indignant.

'That's right, ignorant Eyetie sods, when a man's down always assume the bloody worst, bastards.' To a young priest who shook his head sadly, Beard said, wiping muddy hands on his trouser-seat:

'*Non sono ubriaco. Sto morendo.*' The priest, for fear perhaps of blessing Belli, did not bless Beard. The two Protestants staggered down sidestreets towards the Piazza Santa Cecilia. When they reached 16A Beard said: 'Well, this is very nearly it, Greg. You and I had lunch together at a popular Trastevere restaurant, and then you expressed a desire to see the church where the bones of the matron saint of music lie, by tradition, mouldering. I said: well, if we're sight-seeing, let me see one of the most considerable fiction-writers of our time, who, I am credibly informed, lives at the top of this building. Stairs too much for the poor sod. Heart.'

'Ought to shake hands, I suppose,' Greg said. 'We had some reasonable times in the Far East. Drank too much, of course, but it's many a good man's weakness. Well, I'll be seeing you around, old man.'

They shook hands with drunken solemnity and, Gregson waving and saying 'Good luck,' Beard started climbing the endless stairway. Killing, but that was the object of the exercise. He had the letter for this loved girl clutched in the hand that was not crutched by the loose iron rails that, flight by flight, served as banisters. His hidden eye was twitching like mad. He breathed dark dusty fire with increasing difficulty. Mouth gargoyled to the limit, legs chopped off at the knee, ribcage battered, the devils of the stairway leering and dancing all about, he found himself with surprise outside a familiar door with an unfamiliar name-card: MR AND MRS P. R. PATHAN. He trembled downwards, doing feeble dance-steps, and slid the letter very quietly under the door. But they would not hear anyway. The place, whatever other new or old furniture it had, certainly now had a healthy-lunged hi-fi system. Beard's surprise at still being alive was momentarily swallowed by delight at what this was playing:

> From harmony, from heavenly harmony,
> This universal frame began.
> When nature underneath a heap
> Of jarring atoms lay
> And could not raise her head,
> The tuneful voice was heard from high:
> *Arise, ye more than dead!*

Dryden's St Cecilia Ode in Fisher's was its setting. Beard felt, damn it, quite well and even the twitch had abated. He started to go down the stairs. When he reached the bottom he found Greg Greg gaping at him.

'You still with us, old man? Glad to see you, of course, but after what you said about general condition and so forth I must say it's a bit of a surprise. Anyway, while you're here, what was the name of that swine in Brunei Town who used to be an amateur jockey?'

'Mudd, wasn't it?'

'Yes, Mudd. I thought Mudd at first but it didn't seem possible. Thanks. What do you do now – have another try?'

'That's about it.'

'Well, good luck, old man. Won't shake hands again, a bit pointless really.'

Beard had to succeed this time, for old Greg's sake. He attempted to run up the first pitch, but had no legs to do it with. Hand over hand on the iron rail he heaved hove himself. Always said these fucking stairs would be the – MR AND MRS P. R. PATHAN.

> The trumpet's loud clangour
> Incites us to arms
> With shrill notes of anger
> And mortal alarms.
> The double double double beat
> Of the thundering drum
> Cries: *Hark, the foes come.*
> *Charge, charge, 'tis too late to retreat.*

When Beard reached the bottom again, he found Greg Greg's face working through various attitudes, not quite sure which was the right one: annoyance, scorn, sympathy, amusement and so on.

'Not doing too well, are you old boy old boy?'

'Can't understand it. Could have sworn it would have happened that time. I mean, damn it, you've been up those stairs yourself. You know what you felt like when you got to the top.'

'Perhaps you only feel you're going to die when you're not going to really, if you see what I mean. Are you going to have another go?'

'I suppose so.' Beard lighted a Mercator and puffed deeply. 'I'm sorry about all this.'

'That's all right, old man. One more damned good try. And the best of British luck.'

The Ode was just coming to its end, *allegro maestoso allargando molto.*

> The dead shall live, the living die,
> And music shall untune the sky.

When Beard shamefacedly reached the bottom again, Greg Greg said: 'It won't be bloody do, you know, old man. Fair's fair. Give it another try tomorrow.'

'Sorry about the bloody anticlimax, Greg. Perhaps I'm one of those destined to go out in a coma.'

'Nothing wrong with that. Back to the Grand for us. Death in the bar might be all right, you know. Funny, though, you don't see many deaths in bars. Not from natural causes, that is. Remember Causley in the Snowman in Brunei? That brown bastard Minggu got his knife in all right. Taxi there, look. *Taxi!* Stop, you bastard. Christ, he has.'

Beard had a hell of a thirst on him. Getting into the cab with Greg he was, he supposed, as happy as he had ever been in his life. Nothing left undone, and a whole night's drinking in front of him. The rain was teeming down now, and they'd actually got a taxi.

Montalbuccio – Monte Carlo – Eze – Callian
Summer 1975

More About Penguins
and Pelicans

Penguinews, which appears every month, contains details of all the new books issued by Penguins as they are published. It is supplemented by our stocklist, which includes almost 5,000 titles.

A specimen copy of *Penguinews* will be sent to you free on request. Please write to Dept EP, Penguin Books Ltd, Harmondsworth, Middlesex, for your copy.

In the U.S.A.: For a complete list of books available from Penguins in the United States write to Dept CS, Penguin Books, 625 Madison Avenue, New York, New York 10022.

In Canada: For a complete list of books available from Penguins in Canada write to Penguin Books Canada Ltd, 2801 John Street, Markham, Ontario L3R 1B4

In Australia: For a complete list of books available from Penguins in Australia write to the Marketing Department, Penguin Books Australia Ltd, P.O. Box 257, Ringwood, Victoria 3134.